# The Belle of Ireland

Finally, the band started up, and the guests refreshed their drinks and headed to the dance floor. Delk sprayed disinfectant while Bevine wiped down a large table in preparation for the wedding cake.

"Bevine, you've worked my girl hard enough today. She needs a drink and a dance!" As if it were the finest champagne, Pather presented Delk with a Diet Coke.

"Thank you!" she cried. A fast song was just ending, and the band launched into an Irish waltz. Pather led her to the dance floor. Delk did her best to follow Pather's lead, but she felt shy all of a sudden, as if all eyes were on the two of them. After a quick glance around the room, she realized her instincts were right—all eyes *were* on them!

"Why are they watching us?" she whispered.

"They're not watching us. They're watching the *belle* of Ireland," he teased.

"You can dry the flowers, you know," Delk reminded him. He laughed and pulled her closer. "Seriously, why is everyone staring?"

"I suppose it's because they've never seen me in love before."

Delk stopped and looked at him.

"Perhaps they didn't think I was capable of it." Pather picked up the beat again, and Delk's heart waltzed right into her throat.

# When Irish Guys Are Smiling

## Suzanne Supplee

**speak**

An Imprint of Penguin Group (USA) Inc.

## Acknowledgments

*Special thanks to Angelle Pilkington, editor extraordinaire, Margaret Meacham, kind friend and generous mentor, and Ann Tobias, guardian agent. Thanks also to my husband, Scott, for his unwavering confidence in my work and to Carol Fitzpatrick for the helpful research materials.*

SPEAK
Published by the Penguin Group
Penguin Group (USA) Inc.,
345 Hudson Street, New York, New York 10014, U.S.A.
Penguin Group (Canada), 90 Eglinton Avenue East, Suite 700, Toronto, Ontario, Canada M4P 2Y3
(a division of Pearson Penguin Canada Inc.)
Penguin Books Ltd, 80 Strand, London WC2R 0RL, England
Penguin Ireland, 25 St Stephen's Green, Dublin 2, Ireland (a division of Penguin Books Ltd)
Penguin Group (Australia), 250 Camberwell Road, Camberwell, Victoria 3124, Australia
(a division of Pearson Australia Group Pty Ltd)
Penguin Books India Pvt Ltd, 11 Community Centre, Panchsheel Park, New Delhi - 110 017, India
Penguin Group (NZ), 67 Apollo Drive, Rosedale, North Shore 0632, New Zealand
(a division of Pearson New Zealand Ltd)
Penguin Books (South Africa) (Pty) Ltd, 24 Sturdee Avenue, Rosebank, Johannesburg 2196,
South Africa

Registered Offices: Penguin Books Ltd, 80 Strand, London WC2R 0RL, England

Published by Speak, an imprint of Penguin Group (USA) Inc., 2008

1 3 5 7 9 10 8 6 4 2

Copyright © Suzanne Supplee, 2008
All rights reserved
Interior art and design by Jeanine Henderson. Text set in Imago Book.

LIBRARY OF CONGRESS CATALOGING-IN-PUBLICATION DATA:
Supplee, Suzanne.
When Irish guys are smiling / Suzanne Supplee.
p. cm.—(S.A.S.S.: Students Across the Seven Seas)
Summary: Seeking to get away from debutante balls and her pregnant
young stepmother in Nashville, seventeen-year-old Delk Sinclair goes to
Connemara, Ireland, for a semester of study, where she falls for a handsome young
Irishman and finally begins to recover from the death of her mother.

[1. Foreign study—Fiction.  2. Schools—Fiction.  3. Interpersonal relations—Fiction.
4. Grief—Fiction.  5. Ireland—Fiction.] I. Title.
PZ7.S96518Wh 2008 [Fic]—dc22    2007022972

SPEAK ISBN 978-0-14-241016-5 (pbk.)

Printed in the United States of America

*This book is dedicated to Cassie Elena Paton,
daughter, friend, and* first *editor.*

# When Irish Guys Are Smiling

**Application for the Students Across the Seven Seas**

**Study Abroad Program**

**Name:** Delk Sinclair

**Age:** 17

**High School:** Junior at Overton Preparatory

**Hometown:** Nashville, Tennessee

**Preferred Study Abroad Destination:** Connemara, Ireland

### 1. Why are you interested in traveling abroad next year?

**Answer:** I feel it is important for me to discover the world so that I can become a self-assured, self-aware young woman, and Ireland is so rich in culture and tradition and natural beauty. To me, there is no better environment in which to discover my true self and embrace the simple things in life.

(Truth: I want to get away from my father's child bride—she is only ten years older than me. Besides that, she and my father are having a baby. Connemara, take me away. Please, please, please accept me, S.A.S.S. Powers That Be!)

### 2. How will studying abroad further develop your talents and interests?

**Answer:** The new insights I gain while studying in Ireland will help prepare me for college life and the adult world. Traveling abroad will open my eyes to new opportunities and shed light on what I might choose for a future profession.

(Truth: Ireland seems like such a happy place. Maybe a little of that happiness will rub off on me.)

**3. Describe your extracurricular activities.**

**Answer:** Overton Preparatory Tennis Team, Overton Preparatory Junior Class Activities and Events Cochair, Overton Preparatory Sophomore Class Activities and Events Cochair, Overton Preparatory Freshman Class Activities and Events Cochair, Forest Hills Country Club Junior Social Committee Member, Booth Coordinator for Find It Now (an annual fund-raiser for kidney disease research)

(Truth: As much as I look down on shallow people, I am one. Mostly, all I do is plan events and try to look hot.)

**4. Is there anything else you feel we should know about you?**

**Answer:** I lost my mother two years ago, and my goal is to live my life in a manner that would make her proud and honor her memory.

(Truth: I miss my mother, and I don't think I will ever get over losing her.)

# Chapter One

"Hi, I'm Delk." She smiled, extending her hand to a broad-shouldered girl who was seated on a bench under an Aer Lingus sign at the Dublin Airport. "Delk Sinclair. You're with S.A.S.S., right?"

"How'd you guess?" The girl smirked and looked down at the "Students Across the Seven Seas" logo imprinted on her wrinkled T-shirt. Delk had a top just like it, except she hadn't worn hers yet. It'd come with the official S.A.S.S. acceptance letter.

"That was kinda obvious, I guess." Delk laughed

uncomfortably and waited for the girl to introduce herself. "So what's your name?" she asked finally.

"Iris," she said, and smiled broadly, which was when Delk noticed Iris was missing a cuspid. Plain as day there just wasn't a tooth where a tooth would normally go. "Yep, name's Iris. Suits me, don't you think?" she said, sticking her tongue through the space as if to draw attention to the flaw.

Delk couldn't help but stare. "What happened to your tooth?" she asked. The rude question shocked Delk herself, and she wondered if it was the jet lag that made her forget her manners.

"Congenital defect," said Iris.

Delk stared at the girl in horror. "*Genital* defect?" she whispered.

"*Con*-genital. As in *from birth*," she explained.

"Oh, right," said Delk, embarrassed.

"I have an appliance I can wear—*when* I want to impress people. I rarely want to impress people, though," Iris added. "So where you from, Delk? No, wait, let me guess! Alabama? Kentucky?"

"Nashville," Delk answered.

"Yep, I could tell by your accent it had to be somewhere down there. It's ironic, I guess," said Iris.

"What's ironic?" Delk asked, searching through her purse for rewetting drops. Her contact lenses felt like sandpaper. She was tempted to remove them and put on her glasses, but they were thick as Coke bottles, and unlike Iris, she *did* want to impress people, at least at first.

"Well, it just seems to me that *you* should be the one missing teeth," Iris quipped. Delk felt herself bristle. She hated degrading jokes about the South, and she could tell Iris was about to make one.

"We have excellent dental care in Nashville!" said Delk curtly. "*And* I don't go 'round barefoot and playing a banjo either."

"I was only kidding," said Iris. "I'm a Jersey girl. I know every word to every Bon Jovi song ever written. I'm a Turnpike Rat. Proud of it, too."

"Turnpike Rat?" asked Delk.

"A Turnpike Rat is your basic redneck, only from the North." Iris took a small blue case out of her duffel bag and inserted a contraption resembling a retainer into her mouth. She flashed a now-perfect smile.

"Wow! You can't even tell with that thing in," said Delk, impressed.

Iris laughed and popped the appliance out. "I'm also freakishly muscular, thanks to my sports addiction." She flexed her biceps.

"Good Lord!" cried Delk. "*What* have you been lifting? Small cars? Guys named Guido?" she threw in, a retort to the Tennessee jab. "So what sport do you play?"

"That's sport*s*," Iris corrected her, "and I play every-thing." She snapped the appliance back in its case and stuffed it into her *one* duffel bag.

"You're not gonna wear your appliance?" Delk asked. She preferred to meet the S.A.S.S. director with a compan-ion who had *all* her teeth.

"Oh, I never meet anyone for the first time with it in," said Iris, as if this were the most obvious of choices.

"Why not?" asked Delk.

"Hell, you can tell a lot more about a person with it out," Iris explained. "It's like my own personal Myers-Briggs. I get to see if you're a shallow ass or a decent person, you know, someone with depth who won't judge me based on a congenital defect."

"All this you can tell by revealing a missing tooth?"

Iris nodded and let out a noisy yawn. "You're all right, though, Delk. You passed with flying colors. As long as you like Bon Jovi, we'll get along just fine."

Delk thought how different Iris was from her friends back home, the *West Nashville Grand Ballroom Gowns*, a term Jimmy Buffett used in a song to describe girls of wealth and privilege. They'd sooner die than be caught with less than perfect teeth, or less than perfect anything, for that matter. Delk loved her friends, and she would miss them, but she also needed to get away from them for a while—*completely away.*

At the very last minute, Julie and Rebecca, Delk's two

best friends, had stopped by the house to say one last good-bye. "We promise to e-mail with all the Forest Hills dirt," said Rebecca. "Yep," Julie chimed in, "we'll make you feel like you're being presented right along with us!" They had the best intentions, Delk knew, but the Forest Hills Country Club presentation was precisely the reason Delk *wanted* to go to Ireland.

Every year the club held a lavish ceremony for girls Delk's age. The presentation candidates wore white dresses and attended a formal ceremony in which they were presented. For several weeks afterward, the girls and their families threw parties to celebrate their introduction into Nashville society. Before leaving town, Delk had politely declined twenty-two party invitations. There'd be tents the size of Dallas in backyards all across West Nashville, trees glittering with thousands of white lights, bands playing in the warm Southern night air. More than likely, the combined cost of all these soirees could feed a small country for a year.

*Too superficial* was the excuse Delk had given her father when he asked if she wanted to participate, but the real truth was Delk avoided monumental, Kodak-type occasions altogether; such events made her miss her mother too much. Delk felt guilty, but she'd lied to Julie and Rebecca, told them she wouldn't have Internet access while in Ireland. By the time she returned, presentation season would be over, and Delk could go on with life.

"Left some hottie back home, right?" asked Iris. She was staring at Delk quizzically.

"Huh?" Delk replied, shoving the depressing thoughts out of her mind.

"You had this emo look, you know, like you were missing some dude or something."

"Oh, I don't even have a boyfriend," Delk replied. "I'm just...um...tired."

"Ditto on both accounts," said Iris, yawning again. "Hey, think he's looking for us?" she asked, nodding toward the airport courtesy desk.

Delk spotted an older man wearing a S.A.S.S. T-shirt identical to Iris's (except neater). The customer service rep was pointing in their direction. Delk stood up and smoothed out her linen skirt, which was wrinkled beyond any hope. She rubbed her dry eyes and blinked a few times to clear the cloudy lenses. She glanced over at Iris, who still sat sprawled on the vinyl bench.

"Good morning to ya." The man smiled, his Irish lilt thick and songlike. "I'm Keegin Keneally," he said, taking Delk's hand, "and let me be the first to welcome you ladies to the Emerald Isle." He was a rather compact, robust man with a sharply upturned nose and bright blue eyes.

"I'm Delk Sinclair from Nashville, Tennessee." Delk smiled back at him. "It's very nice to meet you. Are you the director?"

Mr. Keneally laughed. "Now tha-twould be something.

No, I'm just the local farmer, airport shuttle man, and unofficial tour guide. There was a bit of a coal crisis back at the dorms, so Mrs. Connolly couldn't meet you in person. Who's yer friend there?" he asked, glancing toward Iris.

"Oh, we just met," said Delk. "This is Iris." Delk realized she didn't know Iris's last name. "I think she could definitely use some coffee. She's too tired to get up." Iris took Delk's not-so-subtle hint and stood. Mr. Keneally and Delk gaped up at her. Iris was, without a doubt, the tallest girl Delk had ever seen—over six feet for sure.

"Nice to meet you." Iris grinned down at Mr. Keneally.

"Same to you." Mr. Keneally mused. "What in God's name do they feed you in America?"

"Small children and live farm animals mostly," Iris replied drily. Clearly, she'd heard all the tall jokes before. Mr. Keneally laughed broadly with his mouth wide open and a hand on his round belly.

"May I get you ladies some coffee or tea for the trip? The two of you look like you could use it, and we have a few hours' drive ahead of us."

Delk and Iris followed Mr. Keneally to the coffee stand. Secretly, Delk was dying for a Diet Coke, her morning caffeine preference, but she settled for tea with cream, which wasn't all that bad. Lugging their bags, they made their way to the airport parking lot, and Delk was rather startled to see a *very* cute boy sitting in the van's passenger seat.

"That's my son there," said Mr. Keneally as he hoisted

the bags into the back of the van and slammed the door.

"Mornin'," Cute Boy said politely, and tipped his cap. His fair face was spattered with freckles, and he had a shock of strawberry-blond hair hanging over his vivid green eyes. His eyebrows were thick and blond and seemed to have a will of their own, as if they were actually patches of hay glued to his forehead. Somehow, here in Ireland, this had a sexy effect, although Delk knew her Nashville crowd would insist he undergo a thorough waxing.

"Hi, I'm Delk," she said. Thank God she had resisted the temptation to put on her glasses.

"I'm Pather Keneally," said the boy. He looked to be about Delk's age, but she couldn't be sure.

"Nice to meet you," said Delk. "This is Iris," she explained, understanding by this point that Iris would not introduce herself.

"Hey there," said Iris gruffly.

They climbed into the van and settled against the cold vinyl seats. The drive to Connemara was a quiet one. Delk felt herself dozing off, and when she wasn't dozing off (or staring at the back of Pather Keneally's gorgeous head), she was thinking about home—*not* a good thing.

She pictured her dad with his new (and very pregnant) wife, Paige. Knowing Paige, she was probably home rearranging furniture right this very minute. Already she'd had the kitchen wallpaper Delk's mother painstakingly hung a few years ago ripped down, *and* she'd cleared out boxes of trinkets that "simply weren't her style" without even asking if Delk might want them. They'd had a huge fight over that one. Actually, they'd had a lot of huge fights.

Right before Delk's dad married Paige, he said, "Delk, honey, I guess I'm just young at heart" (he was referring to the twenty-five-year age difference, of course). Old and stupid was more like it, but Delk never said so. Her father had been devastated when her mother died; there was no point in torturing him further. Besides, like Delk, he was very stubborn, and she knew there was no talking him out of it.

The biggest shock of all was when Paige announced The Pregnancy. Pregnant! Delk's fifty-two-year-old father was having a baby. By the time the kid graduated high school, her father would be hunched over a walker, and Delk would probably be the one changing his Depends. Certainly, young chicky wife would've found some Ashton Kutcher–type hunk by then. No, Delk hadn't anticipated a sibling. *Half sibling,* she corrected herself. *Only half.*

"Are you asleep back there?" Mr. Keneally asked.

"No, sir," replied Delk, glancing over at Iris, who appeared to be in the REM stage. Her eyes were shut tight, but her mouth gaped open widely.

"So what do you think of her?" asked Mr. Keneally.

"Who, Iris?" replied Delk.

"No! The mother country!" Mr. Keneally corrected. "She's lovely, isn't she?"

Delk gazed out the window and actually *saw* Ireland for the first time—lush green fields, vast blue sky, low-lying stone walls, sheep, and more sheep. It was beautiful. Magnificent. *Green.* Greener than Tennessee even. Emerald, in fact. The van bumped along the rural road, and Delk realized she had actually done it—crossed the Atlantic Ocean and arrived in a foreign country for three whole months, a thought that both thrilled and frightened her. "She *is* lovely," she said softly, realizing how inadequate her response probably sounded.

She closed her eyes and made a mental to-do list: (1) Take out contacts; (2) Nap; (3) Write a safe-arrival e-mail—to her father only, of course; (4) Snoop for Pather Keneally details. Later, she would go for a long walk and get her bearings. Obviously, Connemara was vastly different from Nashville, and it would take her a while to get used to living in the country.

According to the brochure, her S.A.S.S. campus was "five miles from the nearest village." The thought made her stomach sink a little. After all, she was used to Nashville, a large and stylish *city*. She'd lived there her whole life, in fact, and it had *all* the amenities a girl could hope for— fancy salons, massive malls, trendy boutiques, gourmet coffee shops, quaint places to lunch, not to mention Diet Coke. What would she do if she hated it here? Admittedly, this was not a question she'd allowed herself to consider until now.

"We're here!" Mr. Keneally trilled. Delk's eyes popped open, and she was shocked to see rain-spattered glass. The now-gray sky had been blue when she closed her eyes just a few minutes earlier! "There's your home for the next three months," said Mr. Keneally proudly as he pulled the parking break.

"He always stops here on the main road so students can appreciate the panoramic view," Pather explained.

Delk wiped the window with her sleeve and pressed her face against the cold, foggy glass. "Oh!" she cried when she saw it. "Oh, it's...*it's*..." She shut her mouth again.

"It's really something, isn't it?" said Pather. Delk glanced at him. He was smiling at her, and for a second, their eyes met.

Iris stirred next to her. "Look!" said Delk, nudging her awake. "We're here! Just look at this place!"

Iris stretched and rubbed her eyes. "Jeez Louise!" she cried when she saw it. "That's not *Tremain*?" she asked, incredulous.

"'Tis Tremain Castle," said Mr. Keneally. "Your new home for a while at least. What do you think?"

"I think we're not in Kansas anymore!" said Iris. "I mean my parents were delirious when we got a house with a two-car garage. They'll pop a vessel when they see pictures of this."

"Well, let's hope they don't get *that* excited." Mr. Keneally laughed.

Iris was right to be thrilled, and so was Delk. Tremain Castle was enormous, straight from the storybooks—an austerely gray stone structure with mysterious Gothic details—towers and turrets—the stuff of fairy tales. It sat at the foot of a craggy mountain, and just in front of the castle was a large and shimmering lake, or *lough*, as the Irish called it (Delk had learned this from a guidebook). To the right of Tremain was a mile-long ribbon of gravel that meandered toward the castle, but then disappeared in a clump of trees. Delk strained her eyes, but from the road, she couldn't see where the driveway actually ended. Although the early March trees were still stark and bare, the grass was surprisingly lush. A sign of spring? Or perhaps the grass in Ireland was always this way? Delk would have to look it up.

She thought of all the months of preparation leading up to this moment: she'd read guidebooks, filled out forms, and endured a physical. She'd purchased new clothes—warm things from places like L.L. Bean and Patagonia—a far cry from her usual Diesel and Juicy.

Delk drew in a ragged breath and let it out again. She felt shaky inside, jittery, the way she did the night before a test. She *hoped* she'd made the right decision in coming here. At the very least, she was far away from Paige and her unborn sibling and all those Forest Hills girls with their oh-so-helpful mothers and their lavish presentation parties. *Yes, she's a long way from a West Nashville grand ballroom gown,* Jimmy Buffett sang in her head.

The four of them got out of the van and stretched. A light rain fell, but Delk didn't mind, at least it helped wake her up a little. Mr. Keneally hoisted their bags out of the back and set them on the pavement.

"I got mine," said Iris, and before Pather or Mr. Keneally could object, she grabbed the lime green duffel and slung it over her shoulder. Delk gladly accepted Pather's help, however. She had one giant suitcase on wheels, a slightly smaller but very overpacked duffel, and an extra-large carry-on that was filled with random items she'd decided to take at the very last minute—a pair of strappy high heels and an evening bag, an extra hair dryer in case the first one broke, a stuffed bear (better known as Wooby), a framed photograph of her family that was taken when Delk was twelve and had decided to cut her own bangs, a pocket-size dictionary and thesaurus, and a pack of playing cards she'd found in the kitchen junk drawer.

Mr. Keneally led the way across a parking pad to the front of the castle and pushed open the heavy wooden door. He held it back until they were all inside a dimly lit foyer. "The dining hall is straight back there," he said, pointing down a wide corridor.

The walls were painted a warm and welcoming shade

of mustard yellow, and ornate bronze sconces with crystal teardrops hung on either side of the arched doorway. Hanging just to the left was a portrait of a woman and a young girl, obviously from a couple of centuries ago, and to the right was an elegant needlepoint sign in a gold frame, which read *Dining Hall This Way* with an arrow underneath.

On either side of the foyer were two sweeping stone staircases with intricately carved wooden banisters and railings. Delk could only imagine the elegant people who had ascended and descended them. Mr. Keneally snapped on a light, and the sconces cast a delicate glow across the stone floor.

"There! Now we can see at least," he said. "Don't let this place put you off, ladies. It's a tad overwhelming at first, but you'll get used to it. 'Tis quite cozy in the sleeping quarters. Follow me," he instructed. Delk glanced over at Iris, and Iris gave her a wide-eyed "Can you believe this?" look. Delk smiled, and they followed Mr. Keneally toward their rooms.

At the top of the stairs, a balcony overlooked an elegant sitting room and the adjoining dining hall. Its wood floors were honey-colored and gleaming; floor-to-ceiling draperies trimmed with fat tassels accentuated the enormous windows, which from this distance, appeared to look out over a still-dormant garden. Thick wooden tables and a collection of fashionably mismatched chairs had been carefully arranged around the room, and there was a stone fireplace, although it was unlit at the moment.

"Where are all the other students?" asked Delk. She was imagining the meals she would eat in the wonderful dining hall, the new friends she would make there.

"Oh, they'll be arriving throughout the day," Mr. Keneally explained. "You girls are the first. I'm driving to the train station in Galway later. A few more get to the Dublin Airport early in the morning. Tomorrow, you'll have formal introductions. Today is mostly getting settled and learning your way around."

"My mom says I can't find my socks in my sock drawer," said Iris.

Mr. Keneally and Pather laughed. "Well, you'd better learn your way 'round quickly," said Pather. "Mrs. Connolly's a stickler for bein' on time."

"Oh, is she strict?" asked Delk. Her teachers at Overton Prep always seemed strict at the beginning of a semester, but after a while they loosened up. She hoped Mrs. Connolly was the same way.

Pather opened his mouth to speak. "I think it's best to let the girls form their own opinions," Mr. Keneally interrupted him.

"I'm guessing she's strict," said Delk. Pather grinned and shrugged.

Mr. Keneally stopped at a cheerful red door and pulled an official-looking sheet from his coat pocket. "Room assignments," he explained, and examined the list carefully. Delk noticed each of the doors in the hallway had been painted a different color. She hoped the red one was hers. "Looks like this is it," Mr. Keneally confirmed, and unlocked the door. "Iris, it says here you're right next door to Delk—in the *eggplant* room."

Delk's room was modest in size, with dark paneled walls and a slate floor that was partially covered by a threadbare Oriental rug. The high ceiling had been painted the same color as the door. The bed was slightly larger than a twin but smaller than a full, and there was a fireplace and big windows draped with red velvet curtains. In the far right corner sat a tiny dressing table, and just opposite the bed was a wardrobe. There was no closet, Delk noticed, but the overstuffed chair and ottoman would be a perfect place for reading.

"There are boxed meals." Mr. Keneally pointed toward a small picnic basket on her nightstand. "Enough for lunch *and* dinner. Tomorrow morning will be the first official meal in the dining hall. Feel free to look around and make yourselves comfortable. You're on your own until tomorrow, although Mrs. Connolly has asked that no one leave the grounds."

"Are you kidding? I don't think I could *find* the front door!" said Iris.

"It was nice meeting you both," said Pather. He had thoughtfully placed Delk's heaviest bag on the chest at the foot of her bed so she wouldn't have to lift it.

"Thanks for everything," said Delk. She shook Mr. Keneally's rough hand, then Pather's warm, smooth one, and the Keneally men left.

"Jeez! We just got here, and you two are practically engaged," said Iris as soon as they'd shut the door behind them.

"Oh, *please*! Pather probably *has* a girlfriend."

"Well, I wouldn't want to be *her* with *you* around," said Iris, glancing around Delk's room. "This is a bit on the dreary side, if you ask me. I might have an extra Bon Jovi poster if you want."

"Oh, that's okay," said Delk.

"Suit yourself. I'm going next door to my purple slice of heaven."

*"Eggplant,"* Delk corrected, following her into the hall. "Hey, Iris?"

"Yeah?"

"Can you believe we're actually *here*? I mean, we're, like, living in a castle," said Delk.

"I know. I feel like a freakin' fairy princess!"

Delk laughed and shut the door behind her. She examined her new room again. Iris was right, it was a little on the gloomy side, but nothing some sunshine and music (thank God for iPod) wouldn't fix. Delk opened her carry-

on bag and took out a few of the miscellaneous items. Wooby was propped up on the bed pillows—he was too flimsy and worn-out now to sit up on his own. The family picture (pre–kidney disease and pre-Paige) was placed on her bedside table.

She flopped down on the soft bed and gazed at the picture on her nightstand. If her mother were still alive, Delk would call her this second to describe every detail of her trip so far. No, Delk realized. If her mother were still alive, they'd be picking out presentation dresses and bands and tents, like all her other friends back home.

Delk rolled onto her back and stared at the red ceiling. No one *here* knew about her life back *there*. In Ireland, she didn't have to feel left out for not being presented or weird about her too-young stepmom or embarrassed that her old father was having a new baby. She didn't have to watch while Paige slowly stripped away her mother's touches with her redecorating efforts. Except for whoever read the S.A.S.S. application (Mrs. Connolly probably), no one knew she was the sad girl with the dead mother, and Delk intended to keep it that way.

# Chapter Two

Delk had no idea how long she'd been asleep. The castle felt eerily quiet, as if it were the middle of the night, but according to her watch, which she'd set to Irish time while still on the plane, it was only 1 P.M. She wished Iris would make a little noise next door, sing a Bon Jovi tune or something, but she was silent. Probably sleeping, Delk decided.

Delk stood at the window and watched rivulets of rain trickle down the thick glass. She was dying to get out-doors and take in the Connemara landscape before dark. She glanced over at her still-unpacked suitcase and

remembered the rugged new clothes. Hurriedly, she tugged on a pair of Seven jeans (*not* officially rugged, but comfortably stretched at least), a white turtleneck, and a blue fleece hoodie. She unzipped her duffel and felt around for her all-weather boots, also a recent purchase. They were styled exactly like cowgirl boots except in rubber with dainty pink and blue flowers. Delk's father had laughed when he saw them, although Paige thought they were cute (they agreed on one thing at least).

Outside, the smell of rain filled her nose, and Delk suddenly had the urge to skip down the long driveway, an urge she resisted, of course. "Hey there!" a voice came from behind her. Delk turned to see Pather standing in an alcove, his arms overloaded with firewood. "Taking a tour, I see." He smiled and added the logs to an already large pile.

"I had to get outside," Delk confessed. "I couldn't let the rain stop me." She was half bragging about this. Normally, she wasn't a walk-in-the-rain sort of girl.

"If you let the rain stop you, you'll be cooped up all semester," said Pather. "I'm headed home to tend our sheep. You could walk with me if you want."

"Sure," said Delk. Pather dusted his hands off on his jeans then stuffed them into his pockets. For a while they walked down the long gravel drive in silence. They passed the lake, and Delk noticed a row of canoes tied to low-lying tree branches. "Do you ever fish here?" she asked.

"No. No time for it," said Pather. "I did when I was little, though. Ma used to insist on it. Probably just to get me out of her hair for a while. I was a bit of a handful."

"So you don't get in her hair anymore?" asked Delk.

"She passed on," Pather replied.

Delk looked at him. "Your mother's dead—" She was about to say *too*, but stopped herself. The unfinished sentence hung in the air awkwardly.

"'Twas a long time ago," said Pather.

They continued walking in silence, and Delk tried to digest Pather's words. She'd never met anyone her own age who could relate to what she'd been through. None of her friends at Overton Prep had lost a parent. There were many divorced parents, fathers living in different cities, complicated joint-custody arrangements, but nobody she knew had experienced *permanent* loss. "So do you go to school around here?" she asked, resisting the urge to tell Pather about her own mother.

"In Galway at the university. Just part-time. I plan to start full-time this autumn."

"That must be exciting," said Delk. "I have a whole year of high school left." She cinched her hoodie up tight and crossed her arms for added warmth.

"You want this?" asked Pather, tugging at his barn jacket.

"Oh, no thanks," said Delk. "I'm from the South. I can be pretty wimpy when it comes to the cold."

"Ah, you don't look like a sap to me," said Pather.

"A sap?" asked Delk.

"Wimp," he explained. His eyes were mischievous. "I mean with those boots, you look positively rugged."

Delk glanced down at her feet. The boots looked even brighter outside. "Are you making fun of my boots?" She was flirting now, or at least *trying* to flirt. Her friends back home said her technique was so subtle, boys could never tell if she was flirting or not.

"Far be it from me to insult a lady's Wellies," Pather replied sarcastically.

"My what?"

"Wellies. You know, rubbers."

Delk felt her eyes grow wide.

Pather continued, "Oh, right, that means something very different in America. Wellies are boots, sort of like yours, except without the cowboy theme."

"That's cow*girl*," she corrected him.

"Jaysus! I've insulted your boots *and* your politics!"

"I'll forgive you this once," Delk warned. They laughed and walked.

"There's my farm," said Pather, pointing across the empty two-lane road. They'd finally reached the end of the winding Tremain driveway.

"You live there?" asked Delk. Pather nodded. "It's so pretty! Like something from a postcard."

"It was on a postcard once. Might still be, but I haven't

seen any for a while. They used to sell them in Letterfrack, a little town not far from here."

"That's so cool!" said Delk. The main house was a white farmhouse with a bright red door and matching window boxes, which were empty now. Up close there was a dinginess about the place, as if the details had been neglected. The paint was chipped, and one of the shutters sagged precariously.

The stone barn was much larger than the house. Overall, it seemed in perfect condition, except for a rusty tin roof that looked like it had been patched too many times to count. Sheep and cows grazed peacefully in the pasture, and tractors and assorted farm equipment were parked here and there. Delk turned around and squinted in the direction of Tremain. The sun was starting to peek through the clouds a bit, and the Connemara landscape and castle practically glowed. From this distance, the massive structure wasn't austere and gray at all. In the sunlight, it looked white, celestial even. "Is *that* what you see when you first wake up?" Delk pointed toward it. She felt a sudden rush of happiness at being here.

"Doughraugh is the first thing I see, then Tremain."

"D-what?" asked Delk.

"That's Gaelic. Translated it means 'black stack.' It's the name of that mountain hovering over Tremain."

"It's awesome here," said Delk.

"So, you think you'll like it?" asked Pather.

"I may *never* go home!" This was closer to the truth than Delk let on.

"I s'pose your home is a lot different."

Delk nodded. She thought of the traffic and strip malls and gas stations and tall buildings and highways—and hospitals. Pather was looking at her, and she could tell he wanted to know more about the place she came from. "So where do you go for fun?" she asked.

"Tonight I'll probably go to Bird's. It's a few miles from here. I'll meet up with some friends. Have a jar of the black stuff. Guinness beer," he explained. "You could come if you want."

Delk's heart sang at the offer. She opened her mouth to say yes, but remembered Mr. Keneally's words about not leaving campus. "Oh no!" she said, clapping her hand over her mouth. "I can't! Mrs. Connolly. Remember? Your dad said we aren't allowed to leave Tremain. I'm not even sup-posed to be here! Do you think I'm in trouble already?"

Delk wasn't joking, but Pather laughed. "I rather doubt it. Mrs. Connolly is in quite a state over the coal crisis. I'm certain she hasn't noticed you crossed the road. You're right about tonight, though," said Pather. "I'd forgotten the first-night rule."

"So the rule about not leaving the grounds is just for tonight?" asked Delk, hoping this meant Pather would invite her out some other night—like tomorrow perhaps!

"As long as students aren't mangled every night, she's pretty lenient. She's strict in some ways, but she doesn't mollycoddle."

Delk assumed *mollycoddle* meant Mrs. Connolly wasn't *too* strict, but she didn't want to risk it. "I should get back," she said. "Thanks for the tour," she called over her shoulder, and took off toward the castle again.

"I'm a cowgirl on a steel horse I ride," Iris sang, glancing at Delk's boots. "Nice walk?"

Delk nodded. Iris was lying on her bed, a stack of chocolate-chip cookies piled on her stomach.

"I'm having reality-TV withdrawal," she confessed. "These really help, though."

"Where did you get those?" asked Delk. "I'm starving." Iris reached to the floor for a paper bag.

"These are for you," she said, handing Delk the bag. "Some extremely wonderful cafeteria lady brought them up. So where'd you run off to? No, wait! Let me guess. The Keneally farm." She grinned and ate a large cookie in one bite.

Delk sat down on the chair next to Iris's bed and took a bite of a still-warm cookie from her bag. The chips were slightly melted, and the dough was gooey. "I could get used to castle life," she said with her mouth full. Iris was looking at her expectantly. "Oh, all right, I went to Pather's

farm. I went out for a walk, and he was piling up wood outside. He asked if I wanted to go with him, and I did. So, what?"

"So you don't know about my special powers yet," said Iris, "but back home I predict love connections, and I smell one here, right in this *eggplant* room."

"You smell cookies!" Delk protested. "I just met the guy a couple of hours ago."

"Did you eat yet?" asked Delk. She was craving real food suddenly, not sweets.

Iris nodded regretfully. "All of it," she confessed.

"That was supposed to be dinner, too! Now what'll you do?"

"I'm hoping my new friend in the cafeteria will help me out."

After a late, late lunch and more lounging and joking around with Iris, Delk got down to some serious unpacking. Iris hung around in the doorway and watched for a while. Delk found an iron in the bottom drawer of her armoire and draped a towel over the dressing table. "A makeshift ironing board," she explained.

"Cowgirl, this is serious. Should I call a doctor?" asked Iris.

"I just hate wrinkled clothes," Delk explained. As carefully as she'd packed, her entire wardrobe was a crumpled mess (all except for the fleece stuff, of course). "Anyway, I need to keep busy to fight off this jet lag. The guidebook says you should try to stay up till a normal bedtime. Otherwise, you'll wake up in the middle of the night."

"Suit yourself, Cowgirl, but the Instant Gratification Guidebook said I should take a quick shower and go to bed whenever I felt like it. Have fun—*ironing*," she teased, and scuffed off down the corridor.

Around 10 P.M. Delk heard voices. Bags dragging across the floor, muffled voices talking excitedly. She tugged on her bathrobe and stuck her head out into the hallway.

"Hi," she said, squinting at a rather tall boy who was hauling two heavy suitcases. She'd left her glasses on the nightstand, so he was slightly blurry.

"Sorry to wake you. It's his fault," he said, nodding toward another boy standing behind him.

"Shut up, you ass! He was the one making all the noise, I swear," the shorter boy said.

"Are you brothers?" asked Delk.

"We're triplets, and I'm very sorry if my brothers are disturbing you." A girl came up the stairs carrying a box. "I'm Lucy," she said, extending one hand awkwardly. "These are my brothers, Brent and Trent." Lucy wore the exhausted look of a frazzled mother. "Anyhow, I'm sorry if we woke you."

"Oh, I can't really sleep. Jet lag," Delk explained.

"We Devonshires don't get jet lag," Trent bragged.

"That's because we've never been anywhere!" said Lucy.

"I went to lacrosse camp in Virginia last summer," Brent spoke up.

Lucy rolled her eyes exaggeratedly. "You do *not* get jet lag flying from New Hampshire to Virginia."

"I was only kidding," said Brent.

"So do y'all need any help? I'm Delk Sinclair, by the way."

"No thanks. This is the last of our stuff," said Lucy. "So, I guess we'll see you tomorrow."

Delk closed her door and wrapped her bathrobe more tightly around her. It was freezing in her room, so cold she could see her breath. Too bad there wasn't a fire in the fireplace, she thought, searching for an extra blanket. Unfortunately, there wasn't one, so she tugged on a pair of sweats under her nightgown. She lay in her bed and listened to the sounds of the other students getting settled— doors closing and opening, footsteps to the bathroom and back again, whispers and excited peals of laughter from farther down the hall, Lucy scolding her brothers.

Soon the noise died down, and the only thing Delk could hear was the thudding bass on Iris's iPod hi-fi. Delk closed her eyes and tried to think pleasant thoughts, but her problems kept creeping into her head again—her new stepmother and their often petty fights, her future sibling, the Forest Hills presentation, her slowly unraveling house, and her mother. No matter how hard she tried to swallow it, push it down, make it go away, sadness was always stuck in the back of her throat.

Tonight, she was too tired to fight it, but tomorrow she would swear off sadness and put the past behind her for good. Or for the semester at least.

# Chapter Three

When Delk woke up the following morning, she felt like a queen, a very frozen, grumpy queen. She had never considered the temperature inside an Irish castle in early March, but she could now say, based on personal experience, that it was *cold*! In the middle of the night, she'd layered on her Patagonia jacket, more sweats, and a pair of gloves, yet she was still *cold*!

She thought of the S.A.S.S. brochure with all those pictures of lush green fields, glorious lakes, the Atlantic Ocean, cathedrals, wild ponies, pubs, and shops—*in June.* What the brochures hadn't bothered to explain was that

Ireland was mostly cold, gray, dark, and damp this time of year. Delk burrowed beneath the thick down blanket and tried to go back to sleep.

"Delk! Delk, are you in there?" she heard a voice call from outside her door. Groggily, she reached for her glasses.

"Just a minute!" she replied. She opened the door to find Pather standing there, his arms overloaded with wood. Delk was horrified to be caught wearing her glasses, her thick, awful, hideous glasses (not to mention the ridiculous multilayers of clothes—and *gloves*).

"Did you sleep well, Love?" asked Pather, brushing past her and dropping the pile of wood in front of the fireplace. *Love?* Did this sexy boy just refer to her as *Love?* Her heart began its familiar crush thump. Back home, Delk averaged at least one crush a month, although none of them ever amounted to anything.

"I was cold most of the night," she complained, "and it feels sort of wet in here. Damp is a better word, I guess."

Pather laughed. "Welcome to Ireland," he said, and winked at her. "Normally, they don't allow fires in the rooms, but Mrs. Connolly is making an exception this morning. Some students are complaining of the cold, and she's the one who botched the coal order," Pather explained. While he expertly turned the sticks of wood and block of soapstone into a roaring fire, Delk pulled off her gloves and slipped a mint into her mouth. It was one

thing to be seen in her glasses, but she wasn't about to let Pather get a whiff of morning breath!

"So, do you, like, work here all the time?" asked Delk, trying to make conversation.

"I like it most days," he replied, obviously confused by Delk's use of the word *like*.

"Is this, like, I mean, *is* this a full-time job for you?" asked Delk.

"Oh, I don't actually keep track. I suppose if I kept track, it would be. I just do a job, and Mrs. Connolly pays me for it. I trust her to be fair, and she trusts me. The farm is my first priority, and I have classes two nights a week, so there are studies, too. And my family. My sisters and their husbands and children live all 'round the county, except for Katie. She's due to finish up her studies at Oxford. She's comin' back here in a few weeks. Gettin' married, actually, but then she and her husband will head back to London to live."

"That's nice," said Delk. "Are you in the wedding?"

Pather looked at her blankly. "I don't know exactly, come to think of it. I doubt she's planned a thing, but that's Katie. It's all about the books." He grinned. Delk tried to fathom a bride who hadn't planned her wedding down to the very last detail. Reluctantly, Delk had helped Paige and her father plan their wedding, and it was practically a full-time job.

"Do you know what the schedule is for today?" she asked.

"Mrs. Connolly wants students to meet for breakfast at ten so she can go over the schedule and introduce herself and the other staff." The room was beginning to fill with warmth, and Delk shrugged off her jacket. "Don't get used to such a life of luxury, though," Pather warned. "On most days, she'll expect students to pull up their socks quite early—six A.M."

Delk winced. "Are you kidding?"

"Classes begin at seven. You'll get used to it," said Pather with more confidence than Delk thought she deserved.

"I hope so," Delk replied. She pulled back the red velvet curtains. Drops of cold rain were now pelting the windows.

"I'd leave them shut if I were you. It's a mite brisk out today. It'll keep warmer in here with them closed," Pather advised.

"How long will it be like this? The weather, I mean." Delk was almost afraid of the answer. Back home it was spring, the early stages of it anyway—daffodils, Southern sunshine, and newly acquired tans for her Overton Prep friends (tanning-bed tans, admittedly, but still).

"Hard to say," said Pather. "Well, I have a couple more fires to build. Can't stand 'round blathering."

"You're building a fire in every room?" asked Delk.

"Oh, that'd be bloody hell." Pather laughed. "No, only for the students who complained." His face turned red

suddenly. "And for you, Love," he said, and slipped out the door.

Around nine, Iris brought over some warm brown bread that she'd charmed from the cafeteria lady, and the two of them sat in front of the fire sipping bottled water and scarfing down the delicious bread, even though breakfast was in only one hour. "I need a shower," Delk announced suddenly. She glanced at the clock and realized it was already 9:20. "We have forty minutes until we have to be downstairs," she reminded Iris.

Iris shrugged. "I'm ready," she said, glancing down at her baggy sweatpants and mismatched hoodie. Delk looked at her. "What?" Iris asked defensively.

"I didn't say anything," said Delk.

"Sorry, but my taffeta gown was at the cleaners," Iris joked. "I brushed my teeth! What more do you want?"

"Suit yourself," said Delk, jumping to her feet. She slipped on a pair of shower shoes and shivered across the room to her dressing table. Father's early morning fire had died down significantly, and the room was freezing again. Underneath the kidney-shaped table she'd stowed away her beauty products—shampoo, conditioner, shaving cream, body scrub, razors, moisturizers, and scented soap. She glanced at the clock worriedly and put the body scrub back again.

"Do you have a scalpel under there, too?" asked Iris.

"Very funny," said Delk. "Are you saying I need one?"

"Hardly!" said Iris. "But I was thinking maybe you could do a nip and tuck on me. An Irish version of *Extreme Makeover* maybe." Delk was about to laugh, but stopped herself. For some reason she sensed Iris wasn't totally kidding.

Iris was big in an athletic way, but not heavy. Her hair was on the mousy side and limp, but nothing some highlights and a decent brand of shampoo wouldn't fix. Her eyebrows had never met a tweezer, but her fair skin was smooth and blemish-free, and she had lovely eyes and high cheekbones. It occurred to Delk then that Iris would actually be pretty—*if* she tried. "You don't *need* a scalpel," Delk scolded, "but if you ever, like...you know...want a new look, I do a mean makeover."

"Are you kidding, Cowgirl? And ruin this *Cosmo* style I've got going on?"

Delk shrugged as she and Iris stepped out into the hallway. It was even colder than her room, so she jogged toward the community bathroom just to warm up. She rounded the corner at full speed, but stopped when she saw a line snaking out of the restroom. She could hear shrieks coming from inside. "What's going on?" Delk asked a stylish-looking black girl in a pink silk bathrobe.

"There's *no* hot water," the girl groaned.

"Oh no!" said Delk.

"At least we'll be awake after the shower, I guess." She stifled a yawn. "I'm Latreece Graham," she said, extending her hand.

"Delk Sinclair. Nice to meet you." The girls shook hands. "Private school, right?" Delk ventured.

"How'd you know?" asked Latreece. "Oh, the hand-shake, right?" Delk nodded, and the two of them laughed. "You have very good eye contact," Latreece joked.

"And you have a nice, firm-but-not-painful grasp," Delk replied.

Latreece was tall, as tall as Iris even, except in a *Vogue* way rather than a WNBA one. Her robe was elegantly monogrammed, and her hair was twisted back in a perfect chignon. She carried a dainty transparent bag, which Delk noticed held only a bar of soap, some toothpaste, and a toothbrush.

"So what happened to the water?" asked Delk. Suddenly she felt foolish holding her bulky plastic bag. It was no wonder Latreece didn't carry too many beauty products; she didn't need them.

"I don't know. All I can say is this would never have happened in Paris. There's a S.A.S.S. program there, too, and I really wanted to go, but my parents were determined to keep me away from fashion. I'm a model, or at least try-ing to be."

Even in her bathrobe, Latreece possessed a certain run-way charisma. "But your parents won't let you model?"

"My mom is this blazing feminist who thinks fashion is the bane of modern society. My father is all for my model-ing. He has two more children from his second marriage and three from his first. I'm sure he'd like to eliminate at least one private school tuition. Honestly, my life back in Baltimore is a big mess." Latreece sighed heavily and glanced around. "And now here I am in the eighteenth century, where I'll probably end up bathing in a stream and milking goats." Delk laughed. She could also see that Latreece had a flair for the dramatic.

A girl with a towel wrapped around her head shivered past them. "I wouldn't bother waiting for a shower," she advised. "Too damn cold!"

"Okay, that's it. I'll just have to be dirty," said Latreece, whirling around as if on the catwalk. Her silky pink robe trailed along behind her. "A pleasure meeting you, Delk," she called over her shoulder.

Desperate, Delk slipped past the other girls in line. The least she could do was brush her teeth and wash her face. Back in her room she would put on a little makeup and tie her hair back with a scarf. She was sure to see Pather again today, and this time she would *not* be wearing Coke-bottle glasses!

It wasn't until an hour later, after she'd eaten, that Delk realized how hungry she had been. Yesterday's boxed meal was delicious with its cold chicken, fresh fruit, and raw vegetables, and this morning's bread was good, but *this* was what Delk called breakfast! Warm croissants with marmalade and butter so rich and sweet and creamy,

she was certain it had to be part ice cream. There were sausages and eggs (not too mushy, not too hard) and good strong tea. Delk feared she'd have to unbutton her designer jeans if she ate another bite. The Devonshire triplets sat across from her, but there was barely any conversation—by the look of things, they were famished, too.

Delk finished eating and took in her surroundings. The breakfast hall was painted a cheerful shade of yellow, and its massive windows overlooked a garden, although it was now dreary and brown. Delk could only imagine what it would look like when spring finally arrived. A roaring fire crackled noisily in the fireplace, and in spite of the castle's lack of heat, the room was comfortable.

A woman rose from her table, strode to the front of the room, and clutched the sides of a rickety podium as if to steady it. "Now that you've had your fry, I want to introduce myself and give you the schedule for today. I'm Mrs. Connolly," she said. She was wiry and lean with frizzy brown-gray hair, deeply set eyes, and a harsh straight line for a mouth. Her clothes hung off of her frame as if they were originally purchased for someone bigger. "Here at Tremain, I serve as program director and teacher. I welcome you," she said, stretching out her mouth into what Delk assumed was a smile.

Delk glanced across the table at the Devonshire triplets, but since they were sitting down, she couldn't tell who was Brent and who was Trent. She remembered from their first meeting that Trent was the taller boy. Lucy looked up at her and smiled, and Delk smiled back. Like Delk, she was petite, but with dark chocolate eyes and a long straight nose. She had perfect white teeth and a grin that was slightly too big for her face.

As for the rest of the students in the room, it was an eclectic group of twenty-five—some in sweats, some in jeans, a couple of preppy types, and at least one emo, judging from his baggy clothes and tortured expression.

"This mornin' the Keneally men have agreed to give you a tour of the Tremain grounds," Mrs. Connolly went on. "It's quit lashing, for a while anyway, and I think a bit of fresh air would do you all some good. After the tour, you'll come back to the castle for lunch, and then we'll see to it you get your schedules for the semester. We'll also go over the Discover Program and my expectations of you while you're here at Tremain. Tonight, the bus will be available to drop you off in Letterfrack—*if* you choose to go, that is. Tomorrow you may attend church services at St. Joseph's. Church is an integral part of Irish culture, so even if you're not a religious person, you might find the experience educational. Classes will obviously begin first thing Monday morning at seven A.M. Any questions?" asked Mrs. Connolly in a way that plainly expressed she hoped there weren't any.

"I have a question," Latreece spoke up. She was sitting at a table across the room. "I realize this is a two-hundred-

year-old castle, but I wonder when we might have heat and hot water." In a pair of black leggings, shiny flats, and an oversize sweater, Latreece looked ready for a fashion shoot.

"To have the amenities we do is nothing shy of miraculous, but I share your frustration in the matter. The coal truck is here," replied Mrs. Connolly. Some impromptu applause erupted, and Mrs. Connolly waited for it to die off. "I suspect it will be warmer by the time you return, but you bring up an important point. Long, luxurious showers are a thing of the past. Three to five minutes per person. If you adhere to that, there will be enough hot water for everyone. Otherwise, you'll have some very cold, angry classmates."

Delk spotted Pather standing next to the coffee station. He was looking rather amused, as if he'd heard Mrs. Connolly's shower speech a hundred times before. He glanced over at Delk and smiled, and she felt her heartbeat speed up a little. At least the S.A.S.S. students were going to Letterfrack tonight. Maybe Pather would show up there, too. Delk certainly hoped so.

"Last names *A* through *I*, go with Pather Keneally," Mrs. Connolly called out. Pather raised his hand somewhat shyly. "Letters *J* through *Z*, you'll tour the grounds with Mr. Keneally. Have a wonderful morning!" There was a cacophony of moving chairs and rattling silverware and talkative, excited students. It seemed everyone was eager to get outdoors, happy the rain was gone, for a little while at least.

Iris jabbed Delk with her elbow. "Looks like I'll be going with Braveheart," she teased.

"Have fun," said Delk nonchalantly. "Braveheart was Scottish, by the way." Iris made a goofy face and grinned, and Delk noticed she had her appliance in today.

The weather had turned slightly warmer, and the trek around Tremain Castle proved exhilarating. The famous Atlantic wind ripped about the rugged grounds, ruffling the surface of the lake and rustling the bud-covered trees. The gentle mountain slopes of the Twelve Bens seemed to cradle Tremain Castle, and Delk found herself staring skyward toward the rapidly moving clouds and amazingly ethereal light through much of the tour. She had never been a spiritual person, but Ireland could certainly make a girl feel that way. Shrouded in mist and clouds, the landscape had the artistic hand of God in it.

"So, Mr. Keneally, which ones are the Twelve Bens exactly?" Delk asked. There were mountains all over the place, and it looked like more than just twelve. She wondered how anyone could keep them all straight.

"Ah, spoken like a tourist!" Mr. Keneally shouted over the wind. "I'm only kidding you, Delk. That's a very good

question. Actually, the Irish don't trouble themselves with which is which, but you buzzies get mighty frustrated trying to figure it out."

"Buzzies?" asked Delk, glancing around at the other students. There were twelve in her group, and judging by their confused expressions, they didn't know the meaning of the word either.

"Buzzies are travelers," Mr. Keneally explained. "Now, the mountains here in Connemara are just *na Beanna Beola*, or, the Peaks of Beola." He swept his arm around grandly. "In Connemara, you can look all around you, study the landscape from every vantage point—up, down, north, south, east, west—and you'll see unspoiled beauty and grandeur. We Irish don't make a fuss as to which hill is a Twelve Ben and which isn't. Just remember, *na Beanna Beola*. Now you all say it." The students glanced at one another self-consciously and repeated the words *na Beanna Beola* in unison.

Mr. Keneally pointed toward the castle. "The castle was built by a very wealthy man as a gift for his beautiful wife and their little daughter," he went on. "There's a painting of the mother and child in the foyer. Not long after the castle was completed, the woman and child took ill. Both of them died, and the grieving husband abandoned his castle. Legend has it he made his way to the Cliffs of Moher and leaped into the sea. The mist that sometimes surrounds the castle is said to be the aura of grief he left behind."

A gloomy silence fell over the group. Delk had become adept at changing a depressing subject. "So can you tell us about the garden?" she asked, pointing toward the walled-off area just ahead. They followed Mr. Keneally through a wrought iron gate.

"Now this will be a magnificent garden come spring. Already you can see the snow crocuses coming out." He pointed toward a patch of pale flowers.

By the end of the tour, the clouds had gathered again, and rain pelted the mushy ground. The garden talk had perked everyone up a little, Delk included, and in spite of the rain, she was in no hurry to go back inside. In fact, she found herself feeling outdoorsy all of a sudden, as if she could get used to no morning shower, little makeup, mud-caked boots, and every-other-day shampoos—certainly she was dressed for an L.L. Bean experience. Delk glanced behind her and noticed Pather's group approaching.

"Time to wet the tea, I think," said Pather, coming up beside her. His face was flushed from the brisk walk.

Delk felt a ripple of excitement scurry up her spine. "Tea is always wet, isn't it?"

"*Wet the tea* just means to 'make the tea,'" Pather explained.

"I get it," said Delk. "I like tea and all, but do you know where I could get, like, a Diet Coke?" she asked.

Pather looked at her and smiled. His lovely green eyes seemed to draw her in and hold her there. "They sell Coke

at the boozer in Letterfrack," said Pather. "If I can finish up my chores and a paper I've been puttin' off, it'll be my treat tonight."

"Perfect," Delk answered, and headed back to her room. She trudged up the stairs and realized she was humming to herself. Humming was something she hadn't done in a *very* long time.

Even though he was technically off on Saturday nights, Mr. Keneally had agreed to drive the Tremain bus to Letterfrack later that night. He didn't seem too unhappy about it. In fact, he whistled above the roar of the engine as they bounced along the bumpy road. It was only a short distance to the little village, five miles or so.

Delk shared a seat with Brent while Lucy and Iris occupied the seat across the aisle. Like a politician, Trent bounced from row to row, introducing himself to all the other students.

"My mom calls him Tigger, you know, like that *Winnie-the-Pooh* character. It's his ADHD," Brent explained. They were initials Delk was familiar with, as practically every energetic kid at Overton Prep was labeled *attention deficit*. "I have plain old ADD," Brent went on. Delk wondered why he was telling her all this. It seemed like rather private information, considering they'd just met.

"So where are you from?" she asked, expertly steering the conversation to less personal subjects.

"Murphy, New Hampshire. You never heard of it," he said. "It's this tiny town in the middle of nowhere. It's fun there, though. Me and Trent cross-country ski every day after school in the winter. In summer, we hike. Mom says we won't ever have to worry about putting a roof over our heads 'cause we don't need one. I play lacrosse, too. I'm obsessed with sports pretty much."

Delk was wrapped up in her black peacoat and a thick Juicy Couture sweater with jeans and warm boots, and she was still cold. Brent wore a short-sleeved T-shirt and ripped jeans, no coat, no sweater. She glanced down at his feet, which were thrust into the aisle, and noticed he had on flip-flops. "Obviously, the cold doesn't bother you," she said.

"Cold?" he asked. "Oh, I don't get cold. This weather's warm to us." Up close, Delk could see how much Brent resembled his sister—same dark eyes and straight nose, similar big smile.

"So what's *your* story?" he asked.

"Oh, nothing much," said Delk. "I'm from Nashville. I go to private school. Boring, really," she lied, thinking of all the troubles she'd left back at home.

Ever since her mother died, Delk had gotten good at making her life sound perfect. The last thing she needed was people feeling sorry for her, yet another reason not to be presented at Forest Hills. All her friends' mothers with that look of pity in their crinkled eyes—offering to

take her dress shopping or help her father with the party planning. They meant well, Delk knew, but it still made her uncomfortable. She and her father always responded with the same polite but firm reply: *Really, we're fine, thank you.* Paige had offered to help with the whole thing, too, but then she got pregnant, and morning sickness kicked in.

Paige was constantly saying how Delk needed to *talk* about her issues in order to "get closure," which made Delk's blood boil. After all, what did she know? Paige still had a mother, and the two of them were very close. Closure over a dead dog or a bad boyfriend? Maybe. But a mother? No way.

Brent was saying something, but Delk wasn't paying attention. "What?" she asked distractedly.

"Hey, maybe you're ADD like me." He laughed, but Delk didn't crack a smile. "Only kidding," he mumbled.

"I think we're here," said Delk, squinting out the window. There were lights up ahead, and she could see a string of pubs and quaint little shops, nothing like the predictable chain restaurants and sprawling department stores she was used to.

"This is Letterfrack!" Mr. Keneally shouted above the roar of the engine. "Button up tonight, folks. It's a cold one," he said, squeezing the bus into a tight space at the curb.

The students tumbled off the bus and headed up Main Street. "Where's Braveheart?" asked Iris. She shoved

Delk playfully and nearly knocked her over. "Jeez! Sorry. Sometimes I don't know my own strength." Iris looked okay tonight—black turtleneck, slightly-worn-but-not-overly-so jeans, appliance in.

"How would *I* know where Pather is?" asked Delk. "Besides, you're the one all dressed up. Maybe you'll be predicting your *own* love connection soon. Trent maybe? I noticed he was checking you out earlier."

"Yeah, right," said Iris, rolling her eyes. "The guys can't keep their hands off me," she mumbled.

Delk spotted a giant Bird's Bar sign up ahead. She wondered if Pather was already there, or if he was even coming.

"He'll be here," said Iris, reading her mind. They slipped into the crowded, smoky pub and squeezed their way toward the bar. A couple was paying their bill, and like vultures, Delk and Iris hovered over them, hoping to snatch their seats. Delk settled herself on a wobbly stool and ordered some tea (they didn't have Diet Coke, as it turned out) and tried not to stare at the door.

Lucy came up beside them and ordered three beers. "Drink much?" Iris teased.

"This one's for Delk—for putting up with my brother the whole way here!" said Lucy.

"You don't have to buy me a beer," Delk protested. Truthfully, she detested the taste of it.

"This one's for you, Iris—for putting up with *me* on the

way here," Lucy joked. "Besides, we can't come to Ireland and *not* have Guinness!"

"Won't we get in trouble?" Delk asked worriedly. "Mr. Keneally is, like, right next door at the bookstore. He said he'd be back any minute."

"Mr. Keneally dropped us off at a *pub*. You s'pose he thinks we're in here having Popsicles?" Lucy laughed and took a generous swig of her own beer. Delk couldn't much argue with Lucy's point. She drank her obligatory Guinness. This was Ireland, after all.

Someone touched her shoulder a little while later, and Delk turned to find Pather standing behind her. "Hello, Love. I was hoping you'd be here," he said, loud enough for Iris and Lucy to hear.

*Love?* Iris mouthed, and made googly eyes behind Pather's back.

"Hi!" said Delk. The *hi* came out too shrill and overly enthusiastic. *Be cool. Don't go overboard.* She smiled at Pather and tried to compose herself.

"I came with my sister and her husband," Pather said. Delk looked around for them.

"Oh, they're in the back room," he explained. "We've a friend playing in the band later. They don't start up until ten, though." Pather shrugged off his damp jacket. "We had a flat, so I thought we'd never get here. Hey, John!" he shouted to the bartender. "A jar of the black stuff, please." Pather leaned over the bar and handed his money to the bartender. His body was unbearably close to Delk's, and she could smell his musky scent. A crush wave so strong pulsed through her body, she thought she might hit the sticky, beer-sodden floor. Pather smiled, his green eyes twinkling. "Are you a bit shlossed already?" he asked, eyeing Delk's empty glass.

"Me? No!" Delk protested, although her head did feel funny. She hadn't much liked the taste of the warm dark beer, so she'd finished it quickly, as if taking medicine.

"Hey, thanks for the tour today, Braveheart," said Iris.

"I think you have your rugged, good-looking war heroes mixed up." Pather laughed. "Braveheart was Scottish."

Delk was about to weigh in with a smart-aleck remark, but she felt strange all of a sudden—as if the room were spinning around her—and the cigarette smoke was making her nauseated. She'd been so busy fantasizing about running into Pather tonight she had hardly touched her dinner back at the castle. *A big mistake,* she realized suddenly.

All at once Delk hopped off the stool and made a beeline for the door. Outside, she hung her head over a pansy-filled barrel and threw up.

# Chapter Four

Certainly, it was drudgery to have class at 7 A.M., a hideous time of the day, in Delk's opinion, but at least she didn't have far to go. Up a flight of stairs and down the hall. No excuse for lateness, she could plainly see. The castle's main building had four stories: dining hall, lounges, phone room, and sitting area on the first floor; students' rooms and community baths on the second; classrooms, library, computer lab, study lounge, and teachers' offices on the third; staff apartments on the fourth.

The decor on the third level was pretty much the same

as the rest of the castle—yellow walls with beautiful lighting, slate floors in some areas, hardwood in others, Oriental rugs, ornate molding here and there, and windows that overlooked the most spectacular views imaginable. To the rear, students looked out onto towers and turrets, gardens and Doughraugh. To the front were the lush fields, the lake, the winding driveway, the Keneally farm, and *na Beanna Beola.*

All twenty-five S.A.S.S. students attended the same core courses—Irish writers, Irish history, a combined math and science class, and something known as Discover, which was last period. Other than the fifteen-minute break in between history and math/science, the classes met one right after the other. Mornings would be grueling, but classes were over by lunchtime, which left the afternoons for exploring.

Bleary-eyed, Delk slid into the seat next to Iris and waited for Mrs. Connolly to begin. In spite of Delk's enthusiasm for being in Ireland, a Monday morning here felt pretty much like a Monday morning back home, she realized. All she could think about was going back to bed.

"Good morning to all of you," said Mrs. Connolly. While she was passing out the syllabus for her Irish writers course, the sun came out. *Real sun*—not sun blurred by clouds, or sun cut short by rain. *Figures,* Delk thought to herself. Oh well, there was nothing she could do about

the weather, but at least her head had cleared. Now she understood why people made such a big deal about hang-overs—they sucked!

Maeve, Pather's sister, was the designated driver Saturday evening, and she'd kindly offered to take Delk back to the castle after her puking-on-the-pansies episode. Pather offered to come, too, but Delk flatly refused. The last thing she wanted was Pather watching her vomit! On Sunday morning, nearly all the S.A.S.S. students headed over to St. Joseph's Church together (Pather included, Delk learned later), but Delk lay in bed and nursed her uneasy stomach and throbbing head. So much for her great Irish love story. One Guinness and she'd blown it.

Wearing a suit the color of dirt, Mrs. Connolly sat ramrod straight on the long table at the front of the classroom. "In this course, you'll discover what is unique about the Irish writer. How does landscape, climate, and culture affect our written word? How does it influence mood, tone, syntax, diction?" she was saying. "On occasion, I'll ask you to go out and explore the writer's surroundings. The very last thing I want is to have you tethered to a computer or holed up in a library all day," she insisted. "It has always been my feeling that more learning takes place out of class than in it."

Delk glanced over at Brent and Trent, who were seated next to the windows. Brent's mouth hung open a little, as if he'd just been given permission to sprout wings and fly. Trent's expression was similar to his brother's except he had one leg crossed over the other, and his foot was twitching wildly.

Mrs. Connolly spent the remainder of the hour-long class going over the various Irish writers the course would cover. Some of them Delk had already heard of—George Bernard Shaw, William Butler Yeats, James Joyce, among others. When the bell rang, Delk gathered up her books and headed toward the door.

"May I have a brief word with you, Delk?" Mrs. Connolly called after her.

Delk froze and waited for the other students to filter out into the hallway. "Yes, ma'am?" she said when they were gone. Heat settled in her cheeks, and the backs of her knees began to sweat a little. She had a feeling this had something to do with Bird's Bar.

"It was brought to my attention that you were drinking heavily Saturday night." Mrs. Connolly's face was creased and worried, and she had a smudge of chalk dust on her nose.

"I had *a* beer," Delk confessed. Mrs. Connolly raised one eyebrow and looked at her sharply. "I know it's, like, totally hard to believe, but I really did have just one beer. I forgot to eat, and I guess since I normally don't drink...Well, it just hit me wrong." She knew it sounded like a load of crap, especially to someone who probably had heard more than her fair share of crap loads, but it was the truth.

"The *legal* drinking age in this country is eighteen," said Mrs. Connolly firmly. "We aren't so fussy with that, provided students conduct themselves responsibly, but another episode like the one Saturday night, and I'll call your parents."

It had been a long time since Delk heard anyone use the term *parents* in reference to her personal life. "I have just a father," Delk corrected her. "My mother died, and I don't really consider my new stepmother a *parent*. She's only twenty-seven." As much as Delk wanted to avert her eyes from the woman's steady gaze, she didn't. *Look people in the eye if you expect them to believe you,* her mother had always said. "I won't give you any trouble, Mrs. Connolly. Really, I won't."

"I'll trust you on that, Delk," said Mrs. Connolly firmly. She glanced up at the clock above the door. "You'd better go. I don't want you late for history." Delk was almost to the door when Mrs. Connolly added, "I'm terribly sorry about your mother."

"Thank you," Delk replied, turning to look at her. "I am, too." She started to leave but stopped again.

"Is there something else?" asked Mrs. Connolly.

Delk hesitated. "Um...you have chalk on your nose."

"Why, thank you for telling me. An on-the-job hazard, I'm afraid," said Mrs. Connolly, wiping the smudge off her face.

• • •

The rest of Delk's classes went by quickly. History was pretty interesting, and the teacher, a tiny nun dressed in the traditional habit, which Delk had only seen in movies, promised that by the end of the semester students would have a solid grasp of Ireland's greatest wars and most devastating disasters. The combined math and science course was a repeat of things Delk had already studied at Overton, but it would come in handy if she decided to take the SATs again in the fall.

Discover was Delk's last class of the day, and she was eager to see what the course was about. Judging from the description in the orientation materials, it was designed to get students outside their comfort zones, *broaden their horizons.* "Students learn best by doing," Mr. Hammond was saying as he handed out his syllabus. He was a frail-looking man, probably in his fifties, and he wore dark gray trousers, a rumpled white shirt, scuffed shoes, and a crooked bow tie. He paused now and then to blow his red nose into a monogrammed handkerchief. "Learning takes place *in* the world," he went on, echoing Mrs. Connolly's sentiments from earlier that morning.

Trent raised his hand to ask a question and accidentally bumped the back of Latreece's head. "Sorry!" he said. "I'm so sorry."

"It's okay," Latreece whispered, and pushed a stray

piece of hair back into place. She was sophisticated in her cashmere sweater and fitted slacks. On the floor beside her was a Kate Spade messenger bag that finished off her look. There was an uncomplicated sparseness to Latreece's style, as if she were a canvas waiting to be painted.

Delk glanced down at her own book bag. It seemed so juvenile with its pink hippie flowers and smiley-face patches, but her mother had bought it for her the summer before freshman year, and Delk knew she'd never part with it, not even for a Kate Spade.

For most of the class, Trent tried to pin down Mr. Hammond on the specifics of the "learning-by-doing" philosopy. "So when were you guys thinkin' we could, you know, get out there and learn?" he asked, drumming his pencil against his desk. "'Cause I'm ready to roll right now," he said, looking as though he might blast off into outer space at any moment. Lucy glanced at Delk and rolled her eyes.

"Well, we have classes all week, and even though you students are allowed to choose *which* New Experiences you'd like to do, I've already set specific dates and times for those. They're pretty well defined," said Mr. Hammond, blowing his nose for what seemed like the hundredth time. "And I've lined up some local places for you to explore in the afternoons, all within a few miles of here."

"But what about nonlocal places?" asked Brent.

"Oh, that would fall into Mrs. Connolly's domain. She makes all the decisions about those sorts of trips."

"But she usually lets students go?" asked Trent hopefully.

"Usually," said Mr. Hammond, "but you'd have to talk to her. She has to consider the trip educational, and more than likely, you'd have to write a paper. In the past, some students have been organized and ventured off during their first few weekends here. This kind of thing is more on a case-by-case basis. You understand." He pushed his glasses up with his middle finger and waited for the boys to absorb the information.

"That is so cool, dude! I mean, Mr. Hammond." The class laughed.

"I'm flattered you consider me a *dude.*" Mr. Hammond bit back a smile. "I doubt anyone has ever called me that prior to this very instant." He flicked on the overhead projector, and a list appeared on the wall. Delk scanned the items—salmon watching, hill walking, beer making (*not* something she would attempt!), traditional Irish dancing, Gaeilge (i.e., Gaelic), bird-watching, whale watching, flora and fauna, Irish architecture, traditional Irish music, sheepshearing. . . .

There were so many interesting Irish things Delk wanted to try, but her mind zeroed in on sheepshearing. She suspected the Keneally farm would be the location for that

experience, a thought that made her smile. It was going to be a *very* interesting semester in so many ways!

After class, Delk shared a large round lunch table with Brent, Trent, Lucy, Iris, and Latreece. Already they were acting like family, talking over one another, picking food off one another's plates, brainstorming ideas for places to visit, except for Latreece, of course. Her manners, like her dress, were impeccable, Delk noticed. A fire crackled in the stone fireplace, and the extremely wonderful cafeteria lady, whom Iris had nicknamed KC (short for Kickin' Cook), made her way around the room greeting students and asking them if they had everything they needed foodwise. "We take special requests," KC explained. "So if there's a recipe your ma makes at home, just tell her to fax it to me, and I'll cook it up fer all of ya here."

"I say we do the Aran Islands first!" said Brent after KC was gone. He was cramming a hunk of pound cake into his mouth. "Damn, that woman can cook!"

"Cakes are baked," Lucy corrected him.

"Definitely Aran Islands! Everyone at this table is going!" Trent declared, banging his fist on the table. Several pieces of silverware clattered to the floor.

"Pipe down," said Iris. "I prefer to *eat* my Irish stew, not wear it!"

"My bad," said Trent, blushing. His eyes lingered on Iris

for a minute, although she didn't seem to notice. She was too preoccupied with her stew. "Me and Brent'll plan the whole thing," he went on.

"We haven't been here three whole days yet, and already you two want to traipse off somewhere else? Typical," Lucy groaned.

"We're in the Discover program, remember?" said Brent. "That's the whole point of being here."

"I know that!" Lucy snapped. "It just seems silly to go now, that's all. I mean we're just getting to know each other."

"What better way to get to know each other than a road trip!" Brent pointed out.

"I'm going no matter what," Trent confirmed.

Delk smiled to herself as she ate her stew and listened to the Devonshire battle that ensued. To the students at the next table, it probably seemed like Brent, Trent, and Lucy didn't like one another much, but up close, Delk could tell the banter was a sport for them. She wondered what it would be like to have a normal sibling, someone two years younger or older, instead of seventeen years younger, and with the same mother *and* father—all the chaos and noise, all that *energy*.

A part of Delk wanted to go on the trip with the Devonshires this weekend; another part wanted to stay behind and *discover* Pather Keneally instead. However, she

knew if the trip ever really materialized, she would go. Her mother and father hadn't raised the sort of girl who waited around and sacrificed opportunities just because she liked a certain boy. That much she'd *already* discovered about herself.

"I say we camp," Brent went on.

"Where do you come up with these abominable ideas?" asked Lucy. "It's March, not June. I say we find a nice B and B someplace."

"I wonder if they have someplace really fancy, you know, with silk sheets and room service and a spa," said Latreece dreamily. It was the first thing she'd uttered the whole meal except for *Pass the salt, please.* Everyone looked at her. "What? It doesn't cost anything to dream." She took a dainty sip of tea and blinked at the others.

"Tremain is pretty fancy," Delk pointed out. "Well, except for that little problem with heat and hot water. But at least that's fixed. For now," she added.

"It was just a little fantasy." Latreece sighed. She sat tall and straight in her chair. Next to her, Delk felt like an elf.

"I'm all for fantasy," said Iris. "Without it I wouldn't have a social life, but the Ritz *ain't* in the budget." She laughed.

"Oh, all right," Lucy relented. "Camping it is."

On Friday morning, Delk headed down to the breakfast hall extra early. The other students weren't even up yet. She intended to grab a quick bite, then go to the library before morning classes. Since it had turned out she'd be away all weekend, she wanted to get a head start on homework.

Delk was slathering Irish butter on a hunk of still-warm brown bread when she glanced up and saw Pather enter the room. He was wearing a thick cream-colored sweater and a pair of softly faded jeans tucked into a pair of... *Wellies*—Delk couldn't believe she actually remembered the word. She smiled and waved, and Pather squeaked across the floor in his wet boots.

"Mind if I join you?" he asked. His eyes were especially green today, and his hair was still damp, probably from his morning shower.

"I'd love some company," said Delk, clearing her book bag off the table.

"You're up very early," Pather observed. "I'm here this time most mornings, but I never see you. I haven't seen you since..." He hesitated, and Delk felt her face flush. "Well, since that terrible incident with those nauseating pansies!" He grinned at her.

"Very funny!" said Delk. "I hope your sister doesn't think I'm horrible. I was, like, totally embarrassed."

"I doubt Maeve thought a thing of it, and don't mind me. I'm just twistin' hay," Pather reassured her. "Starting trouble," he explained. "What woke you up so early in the mornin'?"

"I have some work to do in the library. Thought I'd get an early start."

Pather took a sip of steaming coffee and rubbed his eyes. "I hear Mrs. Connolly's letting you go to the islands."

"Yeah. The Devonshires planned the trip. We're taking the ferry over, and we're camping. I'll probably come back with consumption."

Pather laughed. "You've read *Wuthering Heights*, I see."

"Last semester," she confessed. "What *is* consumption anyway?"

"I'm not sure"—Pather laughed—"but everybody back then seemed to catch it. The Aran Islands are beautiful. Da and I used to fish at Inishmore when I was little."

"Inishmore?" asked Delk. Admittedly, she hadn't even looked up the islands in her guidebook yet.

"There are three islands, actually. Inishmore, Inishmaan, and Inisheer just off the West Coast of Ireland," Pather explained. "Most tourists go to Inishmore, although this time of year, there won't be many. You'll get a real taste of the locals, and they'll be happy to see you. But it'll be a might brisk, especially for camping," he warned. Delk noticed his hands were red and chapped, and he looked tired, as if he'd been up all night.

"Up late studying?" she guessed. Pather shook his head, and for a moment Delk wondered if he'd been out late for another reason—a girl perhaps. She took a bite of bread and fought off the urge to be jealous.

"One of our Belclares died last night. Poor ewe had twin lambs and died. It's the first one we've lost this year. Every farmer loses a sheep now and then, but I never get used to it. Poor lambs bleating their heads off. Desperate really."

"Do sheep always have twins?" asked Delk.

"Oh no, not always, but twins are typical with this particular breed," Pather explained.

"But won't they die without a mother?"

"We'll get them started on lamb formula. That and a noisy alarm clock should help matters. The rhythmic ticking sound simulates the mother's heartbeat. But a ma is always best," said Pather. Delk nodded. She knew this firsthand. "Wanna take a walk?" asked Pather suddenly. "Maybe the fresh air will wake me up!"

"Sure," said Delk. She could go to the library anytime.

Before she knew it, the two of them were down by the lake—or "lough," as Pather called it—skipping rocks across its surface. Pather stood close behind Delk and tried to show her his special technique for getting the most skips.

"You must be level with the water, like this," he demonstrated. "With the correct angle, you'll get at least four skips." Pather's stone bounced across the surface five times before sinking.

"Impressive!" said Delk.

"Now you give it a go," he said, handing her a stone. Delk flung the pebble, and it sank instantly.

Pather laughed and plopped down on the cold grass, and Delk sat down beside him. For a while neither of them said anything. "So what's on your mind?" he asked. "Homesick? It usually hits students about this time, but it'll subside. S.A.S.S. is a great program. They keep you too busy to be homesick."

Delk shrugged. It wasn't home she missed; it was her mother. But she was *always* this way. Having a good time on the outside, struggling and sad on the inside. A part of her wanted to tell Pather; another part was desperate to forget. After all, she'd promised herself she wouldn't tell anyone here. Delk took a deep breath and looked at him. "Homesick is the last thing I am, trust me."

"That's a fairly loaded statement," Pather observed.

Delk knew she was too far in to stop. "My mom died two years ago." Her heart was pounding now, and her throat felt tight. Pather nodded and gazed at her. She should say something else, explain what had happened, but she knew if she spoke, she'd start crying. Instead, she dug her fingernails into her palm and kept quiet.

"It's brutal at first," said Pather after a few moments. "I was eleven when it happened. I'd go to school during the day and pretend she was home waiting for me. Then, when I got home and she wasn't there, I'd pretend she'd gone off to the market or to church. Two years isn't a very long time," he pointed out.

Tremain's morning bell sounded and echoed down

the hill and across the still lake, but Delk didn't move. Suddenly she didn't have the energy to trudge back up the hill and face a morning of classes.

"Mrs. Connolly is a stickler for being on time," said Pather gently. He stood and extended a hand to Delk. She took it, and he pulled her to her feet. For a moment they stood there with their hands still touching. "We'll continue our stone skipping another morning?"

"Definitely." Delk nodded. The whole way up the hill, she wondered if she'd made a huge mistake in telling Pather the truth. After all, the very reason for coming here was to forget all her miserable, stupid problems, not to dredge them up again.

# Chapter Five

On Friday after classes ended, Mr. Keneally drove Delk
and her friends to Rossaveal, a small town along the Irish
coastline. The six of them climbed aboard *Miss Clementine*,
a giant red and gray ferryboat, and waved good-bye to Mr.
Keneally. "This was such an awesome idea!" said Brent.
He'd insisted they all sit on top instead of inside the warm
cabin. "You won't see a thing in there!" he claimed. "Out
here it's all panoramic views and ocean spray!"

"The view is fine. The ocean spray I can do without!"
Delk shouted above the roar of the engine. Luckily, she'd

ducked into a shop in Rossaveal and purchased something called an Aran jumper. The saleslady assured her it
was the warmest sweater ever made. Delk figured a March
ferry ride across Galway Bay was as good a way as any to
test it out. The hand-knit garment was exactly like the one
she'd seen Pather wear, thick and ivory-colored with intri-
cate cord designs and flecks of gray in the thread.

The boat puttered noisily toward Kilronan, a village on
Inishmore, the largest of the three islands. The ride was
choppy and brisk, or as Iris put it—*Jeez, my ass is cold and
sore already*—but Delk had to admit it was invigorating.
The Devonshire boys were in their usual T-shirts and jeans
(Delk was beginning to think they had molten lava cours-
ing through their veins), and they were having a terrible
time reading their map in the seemingly gale-force winds.
They sat just inside the railing, and every now and then a
salty spray soaked them. With each cold *whoosh*, the boys
howled with laughter and slapped highfives.

"How can they possibly think hypothermia is that hilari-
ous?" Iris grumbled, burrowing deeper into the sleeping
bag that she had draped around her broad shoulders.

"Oh, that's nothing," said Lucy. "They do the polar-bear
swim every winter in New Hampshire. I must've consumed
most of the oxygen in utero." Iris and Delk laughed.
Latreece smiled and shivered.

The ferry dumped the other passengers off at the port

in Kilronan, but the S.A.S.S. students continued on to Inisheer, which was just off the coast of County Clare, according to the map.

When the ferry finally pulled into port, Delk was flooded with excitement; suddenly she was thankful Brent and Trent were too hyper to stick around Tremain for the weekend. The scenery was breathtaking—blue-green water, jagged cliffs jutting out into the sea, a landscape dotted with tiny white cottages and rugged stone fences. A dockhand was busy calling out orders to another worker who had climbed aboard the boat. The man on board the ferry was now tossing boxes to the man on the dock. Supplies of some sort, Delk guessed.

Delk noticed an inscription carved right into the pier, but it was written in Gaelic. "What does that say?" she asked the dockworker.

"Welcome to Inisheer," he grunted, catching yet another box.

The afternoon sun had emerged, and its heat felt good on Delk's face. It was so much warmer now that they were on dry land, and Delk tugged off her Aran sweater and inhaled the salty air.

The beach was only a short distance from the pier, and Lucy led the way with Brent and Trent not far behind. Effortlessly, they lugged a heavy cooler between them, which was filled with goodies KC had packed for their trip. Delk walked alongside Iris, and Latreece dragged behind all of them. The sky and water were intensely blue, and the sandy beach was clean and white and *deserted*. Except for the S.A.S.S. students, there wasn't another soul in sight. Delk hadn't expected a beach like this, not in Ireland of all places. It reminded her more of the ones she'd visited in Florida—Destin or Pensacola perhaps—except without the sprawl. Here, the beach was nature, not real estate.

She glanced over at Brent and Trent, who were tugging off their jeans. "They're going for a swim, I see," Delk said to no one in particular. Iris had flopped down in the cool sand and lay on her back with her eyes closed. Latreece strolled by the water's edge. Lucy hugged her knees tightly to her chest and watched her brothers with the intensity of a lifeguard.

"Be careful!" she called out to them.

Iris raised up and squinted against the sun just in time to see the boxer-clad boys dive into the frigid water. "They have lost their freakin' minds," said Iris.

"No, they haven't," Lucy corrected her. "My brothers were born brainless."

"So you didn't inherit their sense of adventure?" asked Delk.

"They *are* my adventure," Lucy replied.

The girls set to work preparing the campsite: Iris and Lucy pitched the two tents; Brent and Trent stayed out of the way by winging a lacrosse ball back and forth; Latreece made peanut-butter-and-jelly sandwiches for

everyone; and Delk headed up the beach a little ways to a pub for some bottled water. KC had suggested purchasing it on the island, so the cooler wasn't too heavy to lug.

After the PBJs were polished off, the six of them hiked to O'Brien's Castle, the island's main tourist attraction. The afternoon was flying by, and they would have to hurry in order to make it back to the campsite before dark. This time of year the sun would set around six or so.

No cars were allowed on the island, but O'Brien's was accessible by road—for the most part. Getting close to the structure would require hiking up a steep hill. "According to the guidebook, the castle was built in the fifteenth century," said Lucy.

"Good grief!" said Iris. "The oldest thing in our neighborhood is my dad's 1997 Ford Taurus." Brent and Trent raced up the hill, but the girls meandered, winding their way past the maze of low-lying stone fences.

"It says here this was once a fort," Lucy explained when the girls finally reached the top. They sat on a fence, slugging water and gazing out at the ocean. The sun was sinking lower in the sky, but no one seemed ready to leave. Brent and Trent came to sit beside them; even they were quiet, mesmerized, no doubt, by the vast beauty of Inisheer.

"I'm glad we came here this weekend," said Lucy. "You boys were right. For *once.*" She grinned.

Suddenly Delk had a flash of home. She could imagine

the frenzy of activity going on there—the menus, place cards, hairdressers, flowers, lights, candles. Julie and Rebecca and all her other friends back home would be ironing out the presentation details right about now, getting ready for the parties that were set to begin in a couple of weeks. She was so relieved not to be a part of all that, so grateful that for once she'd followed her instincts and made a different kind of choice.

By the time they reached the beach again, it was dark. Delk and the other girls gathered up their things and headed across the main road to the island's official campground site. According to the guidebook, there were clean shower and toilet facilities there. Luckily, the book was accurate. The bathrooms were spotless, and the hot water was actually *hot*!

"There's a place called Tigh Ned's Pub not far from here," said Lucy when they were back at their beachfront campsite again. "We should go there for dinner tonight."

"Sounds good to me," said Delk. "I'm starving."

"What I wouldn't do for some sushi right now!" said Latreece.

"I was thinking more along the lines of an entire cow!" Iris quipped.

"Now there's a girl I can relate to!" Trent chimed in.

It was getting colder out now that it was dark, but Tigh Ned's Pub wasn't far from the beach—across a desolate road and up a small hill. They made their way there and

sat in a large round booth studying the menu board. The pub was crowded, and judging from the noisy conversations going on all around them, most of the customers were locals.

"I'm getting the shepherd's pie," Delk announced finally.

"One of those eat-dessert-first types?" asked Trent.

"Shepherd's pie is an entrée," Delk explained. "It's a mixture of mashed potatoes, beef, and vegetables inside of a pie crust."

"They have a salmon steak. I think I'll try that with a salad," said Latreece. The boys ordered beers and fish and chips, and Lucy debated between roast chicken and the lamb. Finally, she settled on the chicken.

In no time, their food arrived. Steam rose from the overloaded tray, and the waitress, a pretty girl with eyes the color of the Atlantic (Brent's description), served them efficiently. "Shep's pie here," she said, placing the hot plate in front of Delk. "Don't burn yourself," she warned. "Salmon here. Big Bloke's Steak?" She glanced at Brent and Trent. "Either of you a big bloke?" she teased.

"Uh, I would be the big bloke," said Iris. The steak still sizzled, and it was so large it hung over the edges of the plate.

The Tremain students weren't lacking in the appetite department. Latreece polished off her salmon and salad, and she splurged and split a slice of chocolate cake with

Lucy. "My modeling career will be over before it begins if I keep eating like this," she said. "My agent warned me not to get fat right before I left."

"You have an agent?" asked Lucy. "That's so cool!"

"Yes, but it doesn't mean I'll get work. She's sending out my pictures right now. We had a pretty big nibble from this perfume company, but no official offer or anything. It's in Paris, though. What I wouldn't give for that!" She sighed.

After the dishes were cleared away, they settled in their seats and waited for the entertainment to begin. According to a sign over the bar, it was LOCAL TALENT NIGHT. A portly man with long gray hair introduced the first act—a middle-aged Irish lady who sang a slightly off-key version of Kelly Clarkson's "Since You Been Gone." By the third performance, three American pop songs in a row, Lucy was nudging her brothers. "Hey, what about the Irish drinking song you guys got off the Internet? You could sing that."

"We're not locals," Brent pointed out. "The sign says *local* talent night."

"What Irish drinking song?" asked Iris. "You know one?" Trent nodded and grinned at her. "Come on! Do it!" Iris pleaded. "At least it'd be Irish."

The pretty waitress came back to the table to offer a round of drinks. She seemed more relaxed now that the dinner crowd had thinned out.

"We're trying to talk these boys into singing," Latreece

explained, "but they won't budge. How strict are you about the talent being locals?" she asked, pointing toward the sign.

"Oh, that? That doesn't mean a bloody thing! You should sing if you want," she said. Soon the Devonshire boys were standing at the microphone belting out their Irish song.

*Gather up the pots and the old tin cans*
*The mash, the corn, the barley and the bran.*
*Run like the devil from the excise man*
*Keep the smoke from rising, Barney.*
*Keep your eyes well peeled today*
*The excise men are on their way*
*Searching for the mountain tay*
*In the hills of Connemara*

*Swinging to the left, swinging to the right*
*The excise man will dance all night*
*Drinkin' up the tay till the broad daylight*
*In the hills of Connemara...*

Brent and Trent won the talent competition hands down. "What the hell's wrong with the world?" asked Iris. "You got the Irish singing like Americans and the Americans singing like the Irish. Jeez!" She laughed, rolling her eyes.

• • •

Around 1 A.M., they headed back to the campsite. Delk slid into the crowded tent with Lucy, Latreece, and Iris, but she was too claustrophobic to fall asleep. Latreece shifted around restlessly. Iris snored. Lucy, as usual, was the only well-behaved one.

Quietly, Delk dragged her sleeping bag out onto the sand and lay down. It was cold and windy, but she had her Irish sweater and the night's good memories to keep her warm. She listened to the waves knocking against the sand and the rhythmic snores of the boys (and Iris). She smiled and thought how much she liked her new friends already, and how well she'd gotten to know them in just one week.

Her mother would be proud of her, Delk knew. She'd always wanted Delk to see the world. Just after college she and a few of her girlfriends had backpacked across Europe. These same women had made a pilgrimage to Nashville when Delk's mother was sick, and they returned again for her funeral. Delk was beginning to understand their bond. She snuggled deeper into her Gore-Tex cocoon and gazed up at a million glittering stars. "Wherever you are, I love you," she whispered toward the sky.

"We have a report to finish," Lucy reminded them the next morning. Mrs. Connolly had agreed to the trip on the condition that they each write a report on the *educational*

things they'd seen, and she was very clear about the fact that pubs were *not* considered educational. "I think we should split up so we have more to talk about. It'll be boring if we each write about the exact same thing."

"That's fine by me," said Iris.

"Me, too," Delk agreed. The boys shrugged, and Latreece stifled a yawn and stretched.

After a breakfast of KC's homemade coffee cake, they headed off in various directions. The boys wanted to see a shipwreck known as the *Plassey*. Lucy and Latreece decided to take in Teampall Chaomhain, a local graveyard. Obviously, Delk had *no* interest in graveyards. Iris agreed to go fishing with Delk, and the two of them rented a small canoe called a *currach*, donned some dorky-looking life vests, and rowed their way out to sea. Thankfully, it was another warm, sunny day—a light-jacket-and-jeans kind of day.

"We forgot the bait!" said Delk. Already they were well away from the shoreline, and Iris had broken a sweat fighting against the current.

"Well, I'm not rowing all the way back to get some! I'll just stick my finger in. I'm sweet enough to attract the fish."

"Trent would probably agree with you, but I'm not so sure," Delk teased. Iris ignored her comment. "Anyway, I told you I'd row the boat. Come on, you've gotta be tired by now."

"Nah, that's okay. I was *craving* the exercise. I think I'm starting to lose some muscle mass." Delk studied Iris's thick frame. Her shoulders were broad and muscular, her forearms tight with bulging, ropy veins.

"Yeah, you've really dwindled down to nothing just in the week we've been here." Delk rolled her eyes. "I guess it's just as well we forgot the bait. What would we do with the fish anyway?"

"We'd cook 'em, Cowgirl! Jeez, for a girl from the South, you're not very country," she joked.

"Am so!" said Delk. "I like Faith Hill. And Keith Urban. And don't forget my boots," she added, holding up her feet.

"Faith Hill's too girlie," said Iris. "I like that one who sings the song about bein' a redneck. What's her name?"

"That's Gretchen Wilson." Delk laughed. "I like her, too, actually."

A bird dove down to the water and snatched up a fish. "Damn!" said Iris. "Guess *he* doesn't need a pole. My dad would freak if he saw all this. He's like Mr. Nature. He teaches environmental science at Rutgers. Before I left, he kept trying to lecture me about all this nature stuff I should look for while I'm over here, and my mom chimed right in, of course. Two teacher parents—a double curse!"

"So what's your school like?" asked Delk, hoping to get Iris off the subject of parents.

"It's just school," said Iris. "How's that for vague?"

"Hey, stop rowing a minute. What's that?" asked Delk, pointing a few feet from their currach. She'd caught a flash of something in the water.

"Oh my God! Speaking of school. Look! It's a school of fish!" Iris cried. "We don't even need our poles. I can just jump in and catch 'em with my bare hands!"

"Don't!" Delk warned, and grabbed her arm.

"I'm only kidding!" said Iris.

Delk could see them clearly now; they were just beneath the water's surface. The girls watched in awe as the silvery creatures shot up out of the water and splashed down again. Delk was glad they'd forgotten the bait. The fish were too pretty to catch.

When the fish had passed, Iris stretched and began rowing again, slower this time.

"Let me take over for a while," said Delk. She was surprised Iris didn't protest when she took the oars.

"We'll have to figure out what kind of fish those were for our report. Maybe we can do a search online or something. Or ask one of the locals," said Iris.

"Definitely," Delk replied, trying not to sound winded. In spite of how hard the rowing was, she was enjoying the strain on her muscles. She wasn't ready for Iris to take over again just yet.

"So what's *your* family like?" asked Iris. "You don't talk about 'em much."

Delk swallowed hard. "Oh, just sort of typical, you know.

Nice house, nice garden at nice house, good school. That sort of thing. Overton Prep is okay. I've been there since kindergarten. It's K through twelve," she explained. "A little on the superficial side at times. Like, if Mr. Hammond told the kids at OP to *go and explore*, they'd break the speed limit trying to get to the mall."

Iris laughed. "That'd be the case at most any school probably."

"What about yours? Private? Public?" Delk asked, expertly steering the conversation away from her family.

Iris groaned and leaned back in the currach. "Public. It's good academically and all, lots of AP classes, college prep, that sort of stuff, but I can't wait to go to college. S.A.S.S. was a huge relief for me, other than missing the Bon Jovi concert. They're playing near my hometown in April. I sure hate to miss that, but glad to get outta Dodge for a while, you know? Too much crap."

"What kind of *crap*?" asked Delk.

"Oh, let's see—prom, homecoming, winter dance. Oh! And please do *not* forget Valentine's Day! The only time a guy calls me is when they need an extra player in pickup football." This time Iris didn't try to laugh it off as a joke, Delk noticed. "I keep hoping I'll improve some by the time college rolls around."

"Improve?" asked Delk.

"Magically morph into somebody who gets asked out once in a while," Iris explained. "Wanna know my deepest,

darkest secret? I've never really kissed a guy," she said without waiting for Delk's reply, "unless you count holding Ronnie Dillon down in fourth grade and planting one on his forehead. I'm not sure that approach would work for me now."

"Trent might not mind it," Delk teased.

"Oh, shut up about Trent!" said Iris, snatching the oars away. "He doesn't like *me*. They never do, at least not in *that* way." Her face flushed to a deep shade of red, and Delk resisted the urge to tease her further.

By the time Mr. Keneally came back to get them on Sunday afternoon, the six S.A.S.S. students had gone from sort of knowing one another to really knowing one another. It turned out Lucy was scared to death of going off to college and leaving her brothers. As much as they drove her crazy at times, she'd gotten used to her role as their second mother.

Latreece was waging a bitter battle with her parents back home over the whole modeling thing. And her parents were waging a bitter battle with each other, although that had been going on for years, apparently.

Brent was worried that he wasn't college material. As it turned out, ADD wasn't his only problem; he was dyslexic as well. He'd managed to get decent grades in high school, but he was fearful of college.

Trent wanted to take a year off from school of any kind

and travel, maybe work as a ski instructor or a tour guide in some remote part of the country somewhere, but his folks were flipping out over the idea. To them, college was the *only* path after high school.

Delk was the only one without much to say, and she felt guilty for it. She had the opportunity to tell the truth, and she hadn't. She just sat there soaking up the troubles of others, as if her own life were perfect. She wondered now how she could ever tell them her story—*if* she got a mind to.

# Chapter Six

When Delk returned from the Aran Islands Sunday evening, she logged on to the Tremain computer. She had two e-mails waiting for her:

-----------------------------------------------------

**From:** PearsonSinclair@email.com
**To:** DelSinc@email.com
**Subject:** Miss You!

Hi Delk, honey. We miss you terribly. Hope your studies are going well. Since I haven't heard from you lately, I presume the S.A.S.S. program is keeping you occupied?

Yesterday, I played tennis with Mr. Clark (an associate from Testermann's), and I pulled a groin muscle. I have been trying to take it easy. That is, I have no choice but to take it easy——I can barely move. Let me know the news from the Emerald Isle when you can.

Love,

Dad

--------------------------------------------------

**From:** PaigeSinclair@email.com
**To:** DelSinc@email.com
**Subject:** Hi!

Hi Delk! Don't worry about your dad, okay? He'll be fine. I'm the one who might NOT survive his pulled muscle. You know how he gets when he can't play tennis. The renovations are coming along nicely (see attached pictures). You'll hardly recognize the place when u get home! Hope you're having a wonderful time. I'm now officially fat. The belly is definitely getting bigger.

**ATTACHMENT:** Renovation Pictures

Delk deleted the attached pictures without even looking at them. She *couldn't* look at them. She loved her beautiful home just the way it was—the pretty wallpaper with the bluebirds in the foyer, the grand mirror by the entrance-hall table (the one her mother inherited from a

great-aunt), the elegant velvet sofa in the living room and silky Oriental, the butter-colored walls. Unlike many of her friends' homes, the Sinclair house had all the opulence without any of the pretentiousness. *Who wants to live in a museum?* her mother always said.

Delk thought about replying to Paige's e-mail—it would be the polite thing to do, after all—but she couldn't. How could this ridiculous *girl* not know that Delk resented the changes? How could she possibly think Delk would accept having her dead mother's work undone? Paige was trying, Delk had to admit, and she wasn't the wicked Cinderella-type stepmother.

In fact, Paige was a Vanderbilt graduate from a fine Nashville family. She'd traveled extensively after college, worked for an ad agency. She was the kind of girl Delk might've been friends with—had she *not* married her father! *No reply,* Delk decided and clicked the delete button. She did write a quick e-mail to her dad, however. She told him all about her new friends and the castle and the trip they'd taken. In the P.S. she said to tell Paige hi, so it wasn't like she completely ignored her.

That night she lay in bed and listened to the clock pulse its way toward Monday morning. Her mind swirled with thoughts of Pather and her new friends and their trip to the islands. Beneath all the new, *good* memories, there was guilt, too. She felt guilty for not replying to Paige's e-mail, guilty for ditching Julie and Rebecca. Delk wondered how long she'd stay this way, a person she didn't recognize half the time.

In hopes of running into Pather, Delk had come down to breakfast extra, *extra* early. She couldn't believe it was Monday again, her second week in Ireland already! She had hoped her time here would drag, go by slowly like those long weeks just before summer vacation, but she could already tell it wasn't going to be like that. Why was it that good times always went by more quickly than bad ones? She nibbled a warm cinnamon bun and stared out the dining-hall window.

Just then the heavy castle door slammed and a pair of boots squeaked toward the dining hall. KC stood at a long table by the doorway arranging a platter of homemade pastries. "Mornin', Mrs. Flannery," said Pather, kissing KC's cheek. Delk and her friends had gotten so used to the KC acronym, they'd never bothered to learn the woman's real name.

"Get ye-self a cup a coffee and take a seat with Delk over there," said KC. "That poor girl's up with the rooster and not a soul here to keep her company except for me, and I ain't much, I tell ya!"

A mug of coffee in one fist and a sweet roll in the other, Pather strode toward Delk. "Mind if I sit?" he asked.

"Not at all!" said Delk. Noisily Pather scooted up his chair and took a quick gulp of hot coffee.

"Ah, now I can crack open me eyes a bit!" he said, sounding even more Irish than usual. "So? How was the trip?" He took a bite of cinnamon bun and waited for Delk's reply.

"It was great!" She smiled. "It was, like, *so great*. Such beautiful water, and Iris and I rented a currach—that's a canoe," she added. Pather grinned at her. "And we saw a whole school of fish. They swam right by us. Actually, they *jumped* right by us. Oh, and the Devonshire boys won a talent contest for singing an Irish drinking song at a pub there. And we really did camp. Can you believe it? We actually slept on the beach and everything. It was cold at night, but the weather was great during the day, and it didn't rain once! Isn't that amazing? I just loved it." She beamed.

"I'm glad. I'm *really* glad," said Pather. "But I hope this doesn't mean you'll be runnin' off every weekend. We have plenty to offer 'round here as well," he said. Delk wondered if Pather was simply promoting local tourism, or if he had missed her a little. She took a sip of tea and held the mug tightly, letting its warmth seep into her chilly fingers. "Saturday is St. Patrick's Day, you know," Pather continued. "I was hoping maybe to meet up with you in Galway City that night. There'll be a big celebration, of course, and my sister—you know, the one that's gettin' married—is flying in with her fiancé."

"I'd love to," Delk replied, "but do you think it'd be okay

with Mrs. Connolly?" Delk knew Galway was some distance away, maybe an hour or so, and she wasn't exactly
sure how she would get there. Pather had said "meet up
with," which she took to mean he wouldn't be offering her
a ride.

Pather scooted his chair closer to the table and leaned
forward. "I'll let you in on a little secret," he whispered.
"You and the other students will actually *be* in Galway City
for St. Patrick's. Mrs. Connolly makes a big fuss every year
over surprising the students, so don't let on like you know,
and *don't* tell anyone. The name of the pub is McGarvey's.
It's near the hotel where you'll be staying. You can meet
us there whenever you like. Bring the others if you want.
This time I'll see to it there's a Diet Coke waiting for you!"
Pather joked.

"And I'll try to make a much better impression on *this*
sister," Delk replied.

By the time they'd polished off their breakfasts, the
rest of the Tremain students were shuffling into the dining
hall. From across the room Iris waved and flashed a big "I
told you it was a *Love Connection*" grin, but she didn't say
anything.

"Wanna practice your stone-skipping skills before
class?" asked Pather.

"Sure," Delk replied, and the two of them headed
toward the Tremain lough.

Delk picked up several stones and tucked them in her

coat pocket. "Remember, like this," Pather instructed, and skipped his rock four times. "Now you try." Delk plucked a rock from her pocket, leaned down a little, took a breath, and let it go. "It skipped!" Pather cried. "You done well, you have."

"I did?" asked Delk.

"You didn't see it?" he asked.

"I think I had my eyes closed," she confessed. Pather laughed and flopped down on the ground, and Delk sat down beside him. A chilly breeze rippled across the lough, and the bud-covered branches clacked noisily above their heads. Pather leaned back on his elbows and glanced up at them.

"Spring's coming," he observed. "There's no stopping it now. You could hardly see those buds last week. Now look," he said, pointing.

"You're right," said Delk. For some reason those buds reminded her of Paige's growing belly. There was no stopping that either, she thought to herself. She sighed and hugged her knees close to her chest. "Pather?"

"Yes?" he replied.

"Um...do you remember what we were talking about the other day when we were here? About my mother?"

"I remember," said Pather.

"Well, no one here knows about that except you. *And* Mrs. Connolly," she added. Reluctantly, she dragged her eyes up to meet his. He was listening intently. She loved that about him, the way he listened. "I don't know how to say this, and I know it's sort of weird, but I don't want the others to know. I mean I just...Please don't tell anyone, okay?"

"'Tisn't my story to tell," said Pather. Delk tried not to notice the worry wrinkle that'd formed between his bushy blond eyebrows.

"Well, I'm looking forward to Saturday—whatever it is we're doing," she said brightly, eager to change the subject. It was getting close to class time, and she didn't want to leave on a gloomy note.

"'Twill be great *craic*," said Pather.

"*Crack?* What's that?" asked Delk.

"C-R-A-I-C. It means a 'fun time,'" Pather explained.

"Well, I hate to ruin a good craic," said Delk, trying out the new word, "but Mrs. Connolly's giving out project assignments this morning."

"And I have chores," said Pather. "But I'll see you tomorrow at breakfast, I hope?" Delk nodded. Pather got to his feet and extended his hand. She took it, and he pulled her up and tugged her close, so close she could practically taste the cinnamon on his breath. For a moment, she thought he might kiss her. "Well, I'd best be going," he said.

"Me, too," said Delk. Reluctantly, she took off up the hill. As much as she wanted her time in Ireland to go by slowly, she couldn't *wait* for Saturday night!

• • •

"Good mornin'," said Mrs. Connolly. Delk made it to class mere seconds before the bell rang. Still winded, she slid into her seat and shrugged off her jacket.

"Morning," a few sleepy students mumbled back. Delk couldn't believe how awake she felt, and at such an early hour. Her father would be amazed if he could see her now.

"I see all twenty-five seats are filled, so I guess there's no need to take attendance," said Mrs. Connolly. She wore an extra-long navy skirt and a simple white blouse, and already she had a smudge of chalk dust on her cheek. "And our travelers have returned. Glad you all made it home safely. In case the rest of you didn't know, Delk, Lucy, Latreece, Brent, Trent, and Iris were brave enough to venture out on their second weekend here. They traveled to the Aran Islands. I'll expect your papers in my mailbox this afternoon," she reminded them. "I'm glad to know you're taking Tremain's Discover message to heart. Well done," she finished, and smiled.

Delk glanced at Brent and Trent, and the two of them beamed at Mrs. Connolly's compliment—it struck Delk then that maybe they didn't get many of those from their teachers back home. According to Lucy, her brothers had a rather difficult time at school.

"I have here guidelines for your first big assignment in this class, and I've also paired you with a partner," Mrs. Connolly explained. "Each pair will be assigned an Irish writer, and you are to research the person's life and work. On Friday you'll present your findings in a ten-minute presentation. You can even read a bit from something the person wrote. In fact, I would encourage you to do this. The purpose is to give you an overview of all the writers we'll study this semester."

Mrs. Connolly placed the assignment sheet on the corner of Delk's desk.

**Partner:** Latreece Graham
**Subject:** George Bernard Shaw

Delk had seen a Shaw play once—*Pygmalion*. She had liked it, too, which she took as a good sign. At least it wasn't some writer she'd never heard of!

At morning break, Delk grabbed a cup of tea and went to sit beside Latreece. "I wish we could do a French writer," Latreece moaned.

Delk laughed. "It's called the *Irish* writers course," she pointed out.

"Well, the French are so much more exotic," said Latreece. Delk shrugged. Over the weekend, she'd gotten used to Latreece's complete preoccupation with all things French.

"Do you think you might hear something from that perfume company today?" asked Delk, referring to an

e-mail Latreece had gotten from her agent. Apparently, Le Papillon perfume people wanted someone with a clean, fresh look—an *unknown* model—and they'd asked to see more photos of Latreece.

"I don't know. I e-mailed my dad after I got the news last night, but I haven't heard back. Even if I get the offer, my parents probably won't let me do it. Well, my dad would, but my ridiculous mother is so utterly closed-minded about the whole thing."

Delk didn't bother pointing out that they should work on a game plan for researching George Bernard Shaw. She knew Latreece would never be able to focus on it right now. "So what's the next step?" she asked. "If they like the rest of your pictures, then what?"

"Then they'll want to fly me there, meet me in person." Latreece stood up and paced across the room. She tossed a paper cup of tea into the trash bin and paced back again. "I'll tell you something, Delk. If they want me to come to Paris, I'm going. I don't care what my mother thinks. I want this so badly I can taste it. I can *see* myself there. I can! Fashion is my calling, and this is my start! Doesn't my mother see that?"

Delk wondered what it was like to have a real passion. Watching Latreece, she realized she hadn't given much thought to her own future. She was too busy trying to survive the present. Delk was envious suddenly, not of Latreece's runway good looks or the potential modeling contract, but of her ambition, her sheer dedication to something—for the future she'd so carefully mapped out for herself.

By the time the presentation rolled around on Friday morning, Delk was bleary-eyed. Admittedly, Latreece hadn't been much help. She was too busy fighting with her mother or crying on the phone to her father. Delk felt sorry for her, and she didn't mind doing most of the research herself. In fact, she was eager to get up in front of the class and share all the interesting facts she'd learned. At the moment, however, poor Iris was in the middle of a surprisingly monotone description of writer Sean O'Casey, and her partner, the emo boy from someplace in Illinois, hadn't said word one.

"Mr. O'Casey died on September 18, 1964," Iris ended abruptly, "and I guess that ends my...er, *our* presentation. Not much happened after that," she quipped. The class laughed, but when Iris sat down, Delk could see her hands were shaking.

Delk and Latreece began with a short scene from *Pygmalion*. It was Latreece's idea to use a funny scene from the play as part of the introduction, and it worked because the class laughed—in a good way. After the scene, Delk ran a brief PowerPoint presentation and described Shaw's controversial socialist beliefs. Unfortunately, this provoked

a rather heated discussion between Brent and Trent, which Lucy stopped, thankfully.

Late that afternoon, Delk climbed the stairs to Mrs. Connolly's office—she'd promised to have the presentations graded before supper, and Delk was eager to find out her grade. The door was ajar, but she knocked anyway.

"Come in," Mrs. Connolly called. Delk stepped inside the tiny, cluttered office. Coffee mugs were scattered everywhere. Unwatered plants withered on the windowsill. Stacks of papers were piled here and there. She wondered how Mrs. Connolly could find anything she needed in a room this unkempt.

Mrs. Connolly seemed to notice Delk staring. "It's a mess, Delk. I apologize. Every time I swear I'm going to get organized, something more important comes up. You're here for your grade, I presume?"

"Yes ma'am," Delk replied.

"Have a seat. I have it here somewhere," she said, riffling through some papers. "Oh, here it is." She handed the crumpled sheet to Delk, and in bright red at the top of the page was the beautiful letter *A*. "You'll share this with Latreece?" she asked. "Or do I need to make a copy for her?"

"Oh, I'll share it. Thank you," said Delk.

"You did a very nice job today. You seem...I don't know...quite comfortable in front of an audience. Rather at ease in the classroom, I think."

"Really?" asked Delk, relieved to have made a better impression on her teacher.

"I'll have to keep my eyes on you, or you might have my job one day."

"Thank you," said Delk.

"Oh, and I have your Aran Island report, too. Very nice work on this as well."

Delk couldn't help but smile—two good grades in one day. "Thanks, Mrs. Connolly," she said, and slipped out of the office. She hurried downstairs to Latreece's room and knocked softly at the powder-blue door.

"Come in," Latreece called. Her eyes were bloodshot, and Delk could tell she'd been crying.

"You didn't get it?" Delk guessed.

"Quite the contrary. They want me to come to Paris right away for an interview."

"You got it? You *got* the interview!" Delk shrieked and jumped up and down. Their *A* hardly seemed worth mentioning now.

"Stop," said Latreece. She wiped her nose with a tissue. "My parents aren't letting me go. I have to call my agent tomorrow and tell her I'll pass."

"What?" cried Delk. "Oh my God! That's terrible." She sat down beside Latreece.

"It's all I've ever wanted," Latreece whispered into her crumpled, soggy tissue. "And they're not letting me do it.

They're not even letting me *try*! All I want is to see if I *can* get it, you know? But my mother said there's no point in showing up for the interview because she won't let me take the job even if they do offer the contract."

By the time Delk left Latreece's room, she felt like calling the girl's parents herself. She wondered sometimes if parents knew how much their decisions affected their children's lives. Based on her dad's recent choices, *apparently not.*

Delk was sleeping when someone tapped at her door long before daylight on Saturday morning. "Wake up!" she heard, but the muffled voice seemed to come from very far away. "Wake up!" it insisted again. Her locked door rattled noisily. She groaned and slid out of the warm bed. She shivered when her feet hit the cold stone floor as she made her way to the door.

"What are you doing?" asked Delk. Latreece pushed past her and hurried into the dark room.

"Close the door," she ordered. "I don't want to wake anyone up." Obediently, Delk shut the door and switched on the light.

"What's wrong?" asked Delk, tugging on her bathrobe.

Wearing three-inch Jimmy Choos, a pair of tight-fitting chocolate-colored slacks, and a crisp poplin blouse, Latreece paced across the room. "I'm going to Paris," she announced.

"Paris?" Delk rubbed her eyes. "What? They changed their minds?"

"My aunt called Mrs. Connolly and pretended to be my mom. Told her there was some family emergency."

"A family emergency in Paris?" Delk asked.

"I know, it's a stretch. But my aunt said she wasn't going to let my parents get in my way. I turn eighteen in June," said Latreece. "Only three months from now. My agent said we can work that part out. Maybe put the contract on hold until I'm old enough to sign it for myself."

"But what about high school?" Delk asked.

"I'll get a GED, or I'll…I don't know. I haven't gotten that far, but I at least have to try. Just *see* if I can get something like this."

"Is there anything I can do?" asked Delk.

"Nothing. I just had to tell somebody. I'll be back next week at some point. Wish me luck," she said, swooping Delk up into an awkward, long-limbed hug. "I better go. My car's probably waiting out front."

After Latreece was gone, Delk climbed back into her now-cold bed, but she couldn't sleep. All the exciting possibilities and potential pitfalls of Latreece's life played like a movie in her head. *What would Latreece's parents do when they found out? And what if Latreece had to miss out on senior year?* As much as Delk sometimes had issues with her school, she couldn't imagine not graduating with all her friends.

After an hour of tossing and turning, Delk figured she might as well get up. There was no point fretting over Latreece's life when she couldn't even fix her own. Besides, today was St. Patrick's Day and she still had to pack an overnight bag, as per Mrs. Connolly's orders, and meet the other S.A.S.S. students in the lobby by 6 A.M.

Delk threw on a pair of jeans and a turtleneck and headed down the hall to Lucy's room. Lucy swung open the bright yellow door and tipped her hat dramatically. "Top a the mornin' to ya," she said in her best Irish brogue. She was wearing lime green sneakers, army green cargo pants, and a bright green T-shirt that said *Kiss me I'm Irish*—and she clutched a homemade top hat decorated with fake gold coins and rainbow stickers.

"Wow!" said Delk. "You look great! I can't believe we're actually in Ireland on St. Patrick's Day!"

"I know," Lucy replied. "I was up half the night planning my outfit. Actually, that's a lie. I had it planned before I even left New Hampshire. Dorkish, I realize. Speaking of dorks, let's go check out my brothers." She grinned.

"Wait! You have to help *me* first!" Delk pleaded. "I don't have anything green!" She sat on the bed while Lucy rummaged through a pile of clothes. Finally, they settled on a slightly wrinkled sage-green blouse and a darker green headband. Delk's outfit didn't have quite the punchy effect as Lucy's, but it was better than nothing.

"Do you think we're overdressed?" asked Delk, staring

at her reflection in the mirror. "We're not too green, are we? I don't want to look like a tourist."

"Next to my brothers, we'll look completely normal, trust me. They're both going as that leprachaun from the Lucky Charms cereal commercial."

"Oh no," Delk groaned.

"At least you're not related to them!" said Lucy. "I think they just do this sort of thing to humiliate me."

A little before six, Delk, Lucy, and Iris made their way to the foyer. Horsing around behind them were the leprechauns, Brent and Trent.

"Frosted Lucky Charms, they're magically delicious!" Brent started.

"They're always after me Lucky Charms," Trent added.

"You're both ridiculous," said Lucy.

"Total idiots," Iris agreed, tugging at her cap, which was designed to resemble the Irish flag.

"You losers would be so bored without us," said Trent. "Admit it, Luce." He nudged his sister playfully. Lucy rolled her eyes and turned her attention to Mrs. Connolly, who stood on the stairs trying to get the students to be quiet.

"I've called this morning's meeting to announce a little surprise for you all," said Mrs. Connolly tightly. "We're going to celebrate St. Patrick's Day in an authentic manner by making a pilgrimage to Croagh Patrick, the mountain where Saint Patrick fasted for forty long days."

"I thought people went to *parades* on St. Patrick's Day?"

Trent mumbled under his breath. Delk nudged him to get quiet, and wondered if Lucy's mothering tendencies might be rubbing off on her.

The group trickled out into the cold morning air and climbed the steps to the warm bus. Mr. Keneally had left it running for a while and cranked the heat up.

"Who's gonna see our costumes on a mountain?" Brent complained, plopping down in a seat by himself.

"Hopefully nobody," said Lucy.

Quietly, Delk climbed in next to Iris. *What about Galway City?* she wondered. *And what about meeting up with Pather and his sister and her fiancé?* Maybe Pather had gotten the Tremain plans mixed up, or perhaps Mrs. Connolly had changed her mind. Or, maybe they were going to Croagh Patrick first and then heading to Galway later? "Where do you think we're spending the night?" Delk asked Iris.

"Beats the hell outta me. Somewhere on that mountain, I guess. Think they sell green beer there?"

Delk shrugged. It wasn't the green beer she was worried about.

# Chapter Seven

The sky was laden with threatening clouds when they got off the bus in County Mayo less than an hour later. It was just before sunrise, when the world has that eerie, ghostly glow, and it was chilly. Delk tugged on her jacket and shifted her weight from one foot to the other to try to warm up. In spite of her worries as to how the day's plans would turn out, she had to admit the sights at the foot of Croagh Patrick were tremendous—vast open landscape, hazy fog hovering just above the damp ground. She could only imagine how beautiful things would be up top.

"*Croagh* actually means 'mound,'" Mrs. Connolly was

explaining, and in Gaeilge it's called *Cruaic Aigli*. The locals call the mountain the Reek, but the rest of the world knows it as Croagh Patrick. You can see this will be a rather arduous climb, but I think we can do it fairly quickly. Two hours up, at the most. Even less coming down. And you're all young!" she pointed out. "We'll take a look at the statue of Saint Patrick when we come back down again."

"Jeez, these Irish people like to get up early!" Iris grumbled. "The sun isn't even up yet!"

"I'm starting to get used to it," said Delk, stuffing her hands into her pockets.

"Yeah, well, that might have something to do with your little daily breakfast date. If I had some hottie to meet every morning, I'd get up all bright-eyed and bushy-tailed, too. Now look at *them*!" Iris pointed ahead to Brent, Trent, and Lucy. The three Devonshires were heading up the mountain at record speed. Lucy was slightly behind her brothers, but not by much, and already they were far ahead of the group. "I've decided their mom must've been hungry during labor," said Iris.

"Why's that?" asked Delk, anticipating a joke. She could always tell when Iris was about to say something smart-alecky. Her eyes got narrower, and she bit her lip slightly.

"She named her kids BLT, for cryin' out loud!" said Iris. "Brent, Lucy, and Trent—*B-L-T*. I wonder if anybody's ever noticed that before?"

"You are *so* obsessed with food," said Delk.

"What I wouldn't give for a BLT right now," said Iris. "A big fat one with homegrown Jersey tomatoes, not those rank kind in the store, like in December. All pale and fake, no taste at all." She paused. "I bet KC would make a kickin' BLT!"

"Shut *up!*" said Delk. "You're making me hungry."

"So how *is* the romance?" asked Iris.

"You mean the one between you and Trent? How would *I* know?" Delk teased.

"Trent does *not* like me," Iris replied, rolling her eyes.

"It's not really a romance. We're just friends. Pather is sweet, and he...well, he's the sort of guy you can really talk to, you know?"

"I wouldn't know. Like I said, most guys don't talk to me," said Iris. "Unless it's about sports. Or, once this guy noticed my Bon Jovi T-shirt, and he came up to me and said he was a fan, too. God, it was so romantic!" She pretended to swoon.

Delk hesitated. She wondered if she should dig deeper into the subject or just let it go. She decided to dig. "So why wouldn't guys talk to you?"

"I'm not exactly a candidate for *The Bachelor*," said Iris.

"You don't have to look like a TV star to get a date."

"You shouldn't look like a bouncer either!"

"You don't look like a bouncer," Delk protested. "I think you're just scared." She meant it as a challenge, but Iris shrugged it off.

"I am what I am," said Iris. "Sometimes the jock-girl thing works out okay, you know? Like on a ball field or a court of some kind, I kick total ass. Other times, it's not so good. I guess you gotta take what life gives and make lemonade or something like that."

"That's lemons!" said Delk. "And *you* are *not* a lemon! I have an idea, though. You could let me do a makeover on you. Nothing drastic, just subtle changes here and there."

"That'd make it worse."

"How?" asked Delk.

"Because if I looked my best and guys still blew me off, that'd suck even more!"

"Come on," said Delk. "It'd be fun."

"Oh yeah. A real hoot," Iris groaned.


Delk was surprised when they finally reached the summit. She and Iris were so busy talking, she hadn't noticed how close to the top they were getting.

"What took you so long?" Trent teased. He sat chugging water in his green leprechaun suit.

"Not everybody has rainbow access," said Iris. Trent laughed.

Delk glanced around and tried to take in the spectacular view—the water, the sky, the tiny cottages dotting the lush, green landscape below. She thought of taking a picture, but it seemed pointless. No picture could do it justice—or capture the feeling in Delk's heart. She had *so* made the right decision in coming here! So, so, so, so, *so* made the right decision!

"For the most part, I just want all of you to enjoy this view," said Mrs. Connolly. "But I would like to tell you a little bit about Saint Patrick. We are so accustomed to parades and beer and shamrocks, and that is part of the Irish tradition, but it's also important to know where our traditions come from, how they evolved, who they honor." Delk stepped closer to Mrs. Connolly so she could hear above the rush of wind whistling in her ears. She wondered how St. Paddy's Day could possibly be associated with this beautiful mountain.

"Now the legend of St. Patrick is that he was called here to this holy mountain by God, and his task was to drive all the snakes out of Ireland." Delk glanced down at her feet. She certainly hoped the saint had been successful! "But this was actually just a metaphor," Mrs. Connolly went on. "Does anybody know what it actually means?"

Lucy quickly raised her hand. "The story is about the natives' conversion to Christianity. God supposedly called on Patrick to come and save the Irish people by passing on the Christian faith. And Patrick banished the Druids. The Druids were pagans, and their symbol was the snake. That's where the snake metaphor comes from."

"You know your history, I see," Mrs. Connolly observed.

"My dad's a big history buff." Lucy's face flushed bright red, and Brent and Trent looked at their sister approvingly. Clearly, they were proud of her.

"Well, it's impressive," said Mrs. Connolly. "Okay, let's soak up the view a bit longer, and then we'd better get moving. I want you all to get a good look at Saint Patrick's statue down below, and we have more travels ahead of us today."

Delk felt hope rise in her chest. Maybe they were going to Galway City, after all!

When they reached the statue and Mrs. Connolly announced their plans for the rest of St. Patrick's Day—the parade in Galway City in the afternoon, supper that evening at the hotel where they'd be staying, and a night of pubs and Irish music—Delk tried to look surprised. She couldn't wait to see Pather and meet his sister and future brother-in-law. Hopefully, she could shower after the parade and freshen up a bit before their date. *Was this a date?* she wondered. *Or just him being friendly?*

It was nearly two hours later when the S.A.S.S. students piled off the bus and stepped out into the Galway City sunshine. The sky had gone from rainy and cloudy to clear and sunny, all within a single morning. The temperature had risen slightly, too, so Delk took off her jacket and tied it around her waist. The parade was about to begin, so there wasn't time to unload the bags at the hotel.

Luckily, Delk had packed lightly. Everything fit neatly into her backpack—a change of clothes, a toothbrush, some underwear, her makeup bag, and a spare pair of contact lenses (just in case). Maybe the hotel would have an iron so she could press the wrinkled green blouse she'd borrowed from Lucy.

Bands played, whistles blew, music blared out of pubs, and already a few of the locals were drinking Guinness. The Galway parade hadn't started yet, but the excitement in the air indicated it was about to. Delk and Lucy positioned themselves in front of Iris and Brent so they could actually *see* the parade, and Trent went off in search of snacks for Iris.

The theme of the parade was Saint Patrick's heroic struggle to save the Irish. Kicking off the exhibition was a colorful papier-mâché float. It graphically depicted Saint Patrick awaking from his dream—his alarmed reaction to the call from God. Interspersed between themed floats were the typical parade sights, marching bands, cheerleaders, local politicians, and even bagpipes. Later, there was a series of four floats, one after the other, which portrayed the saint's forty days of fasting, and still another of his battle with the snakes, and finally a float made entirely of clover, which showed the Druids' defeat.

Delk was glad Mrs. Connolly had made them trek up that mountain. At least now she understood the significance of what she was seeing. She felt guilty for complaining.

It occurred to her how difficult it must be to teach. Delk's history teacher back at OP always said, *So much to learn! So much resistance to learning!* And it was true. Delk was guilty of this resistance herself at times. She supposed most students were, except for maybe Lucy.

When the parade finally ended a couple of hours later, the twenty-five weary students began the rather long walk to their hotel. Delk was so relieved when they finally got there. Her back was aching, and she was desperate for a shower and a nap. She, Iris, and Lucy shared a small room with two beds and a cot, and the boys took a room right next door. The rest of the students were scattered all over the hotel. "So what's on the agenda tonight ladies?" asked Lucy. "Pubs, dancing, and green beer?" Her hair was freshly washed, and she stood wrapped up in a towel.

Delk hesitated. "I'm meeting Pather at a place called McGarvey's. His sister and her fiancé have flown in from London." She tried to make her plans sound casual, but Iris and Lucy blinked at her.

"Meetin' the fam, I see," said Iris.

"It's not like *that*! Y'all are welcome to come, too," Delk added. Lucy and Iris exchanged looks.

"I think we'll pass, Cowgirl. This could be the night of the hookup." She winked.

"I'm not hooking up! He hasn't even kissed me yet," Delk protested.

"Aha! You said *yet*. Y-E-T!" Iris teased.

"You did say *yet*," Lucy agreed.

Iris and Lucy walked with Delk to McGarvey's, but they didn't bother coming inside once they saw Pather and his sister and her fiancé settled at a cozy booth by the window. They were meeting the boys and several other S.A.S.S. students at a pub down the street.

Delk felt shy all of a sudden, but she ducked inside the door and made her way to Pather's table. "Hello, Love!" he said, and kissed her cheek. "This is Katie, my fancy Oxford sister. Katie, this is Delk," he said. "And this fine man is Seamus!"

"You didn't tell me I had a twin!" said Katie. Their resemblance to each other was striking: same dark hair (although Katie's was curly); similar fair skin tones; they both had light-colored eyes—Katie's a crisp blue, Delk's a stormy gray. "I'm twenty-seven, though, an old lady compared to you!" Katie laughed.

"And soon you'll be *my* old lady!" Seamus joked, and hugged Katie tightly. Katie shoved him playfully.

Delk slid into the booth beside Pather, and he put his arm around her. She could feel it on the ridge of the seat just above her shoulders. He wasn't actually touching her, but there was a certain protectiveness in the gesture.

"Well, all I can say is it's nice to *finally* meet the girl I've

heard so much about," said Katie, winking at her brother. Pather's face flushed a deep shade of red, but he didn't say anything. "So how do you like Ireland so far? You're not bored living in the country, so far away from Starbucks and The Gap?"

Delk laughed. "Hardly!" she replied. "I've...well, I haven't fallen in love with a *place* since I was six and my parents took me to Disney World," she said. "But Ireland is so great. The countryside and lush colors and *na Beanna Beola* and so much open space. I'm from Tennessee, which everybody in America thinks of as this sort of bucolic, hillbilly place, but Nashville is very different from that. It's a city. I think I could stay in Ireland forever!"

"You sound like my brother. You should hear Pather go on and on about the fact that *we* live in a city. It's going to kill 'im when he moves to Galway in the fall. I expect you'll be right back in Connemara every chance you get," said Katie.

Pather grinned and nodded. "I'm a fan of wide, open spaces."

"Look," said Seamus, "the band is startin' up. Let's get a dance in, shall we?" He looked at Katie.

Soon the music was blaring, and Delk and Pather had the booth to themselves. "Is it hard for you to think about leaving the farm?" She shouted over the noise.

"Desperately," said Pather. "It's not just the farm, though. It's Da, too. He's alone so much of the time. 'Tis a worry. The whole family's around, but I'm the only one who really helps on the farm. All my sisters are either raising families, or they have jobs, or both. I worry how he'll manage on his own. What about *your* father?"

Delk felt herself stiffen at the question. She'd gotten so used to avoiding the subject it took her a second to realize that with Pather she didn't have to. "He's remarried," she said.

"Do you like her?" Pather asked.

"She's twenty-seven. Daddy's fifty-two. It's weird." The volume rose even louder, and Delk felt herself trail off. It was too noisy to talk about important things.

"You two go dance now," Katie insisted when she and Seamus returned. "We'll stay here and make sure no one takes our snug." Delk assumed *snug* meant "booth."

Pather led her to the dance floor, where they were supposed to be doing something called the "Galway reel." The bandleader was calling out the steps: take hands, advance for two, return for two, turn around for two, sidestep right, blah, blah, blah. Delk glanced up to see if Pather was embarrassed to be dancing with her—she wasn't exactly *skilled* at the Galway reel—but he seemed too preoccupied with his own footwork to notice hers.

When the reel was finally over, Pather yelled into her ear, "Wanna get away from this hooley for a while?"

"Sure," she replied, even though she had no idea what a *hooley* was. While Pather went to tell Katie and Seamus

they were going out for a bit, Delk waited by the door. The bar was even more crowded now, and she was anxious suddenly to get outdoors.

"This is Shop Street," said Pather when they made it outside.

"Let me guess, there are shops here!" Delk teased.

"Not only is she pretty, she's clever, too!" said Pather. Delk punched his arm playfully, and Pather latched on to her hand. A surge of energy tingled up Delk's arm. "Abbey Gate Street eventually turns into Smith," Pather explained. "The Salmon Weir Bridge isn't too far from here. We'll head in that direction."

There were still hordes of people out—the St. Patrick's celebration seemed far from over. Delk imagined Brent and Trent must be feeling pretty goofy in their leprechaun costumes (or, more likely, Lucy was feeling goofy about their costumes). The Irish children wore lots of green, Delk had noticed, but for the most part, the adults stuck to something called "the wearing of the shamrock." They simply pinned a shamrock to their regular clothing. Certainly, there were no leprechauns, other than the ones *in* the parade.

The Irish pubs didn't serve green beer either. Delk had expected the streets to be flowing with the stuff, but it turned out this was an American tradition, not an Irish one. The beer on St. Paddy's Day was the same color as any other day. Instead, the pubs made something called a "shamrock shake," a green-tinted milk shake. According to the waitress at the hotel restaurant, the traditional meal for St. Paddy's in Ireland was something called bacon and cabbage, except the Irish term *bacon* really meant corned beef, and what Delk thought of as regular crispy bacon, the Irish referred to as *rashers*. Confusing to say the least!

Except for a few cars crossing over now and then, the bridge was empty. Delk could hear water rushing beneath them, feel the coolness rising off the river. "What's that?" she asked, pointing toward a domed structure.

"Oh, that's the Cathedral of St. Nicholas," Pather explained.

"It's lovely," said Delk. "It's so quiet here. It's nice."

"I agree. The big packed bar scene always sounds great until I get there, but I'm not much on shoutin' across a table and knockin' into people on the dance floor. Katie thinks I'm turning into an old man. She'll be relieved when I go off to college, I think."

"Why?" asked Delk.

"She worries I'm too attached to the farm. Says it'll be good for me to meet some new friends. It's the Oxford mentality perhaps. I wouldn't know. The truth is, I'm happy where I am. Katie can be a bit bossy," he said. "Do you have siblings?"

"I'm an only child," said Delk.

"Really? An only child? Growing up, I shared a bathroom with five sisters. Until recently, I couldn't imagine having space to myself." He laughed.

**113**

"Until recently, I couldn't imagine *not* having a space to myself, especially a bathroom. Sharing isn't so bad, I guess. It'll get me ready for the whole college dorm scene." Delk hesitated, wondering if she should bring up the *rest* of the story. "My dad's wife is pregnant, though," she added finally.

"You don't look happy about that," said Pather.

"It was the final thing that nudged me into coming here."

"There were a whole list of troubles, then?" Delk loved the way Pather's accent had a swing to it—up on the last syllable instead of down.

"The marriage to Paige was one. Then Paige decided to completely redo our house. My mother's house, I should say. Most of our furniture is stuff my mom inherited. And there was the baby news. Oh, yes, and the Forest Hills presentation."

"Presentation?"

"It's this, like, big party when you're presented into the whole country-club social world. You're considered a real adult. It's sort of silly, but it's a big deal in my hometown. You definitely need a mother around to plan something like that."

"Well, even if you don't care for your stepma, it'll be great fun to have a dote, don't you think? A baby, that is. I have twelve nieces and nephews, and since I'm so much older, they all think I'm a hero. It's a great boost for one's ego."

"Christmas must be insane at your house."

"When we were little, every day was insane!"

"It would've been fun to...you know...have a *real* sibling, I guess, but this one just feels like...well, like my replacement." Delk couldn't believe she was saying these things out loud. She barely let herself think them, much less tell someone else.

Pather stared at her, his face serious now. The worry wrinkle was between his eyebrows again. "Do you think Paige could ever replace your ma?" he asked.

"Not in a million years!" said Delk, horrified. "No one could!"

Pather pulled her closer. "Then what makes you think a new child could ever replace an older one? One sibling doesn't cancel out another."

"I guess I never thought of it like that," said Delk.

"And it's easy for me to say. Da never remarried, so I don't know what it feels like to stand in your—er—cowgirl boots." He grinned at her. She liked the way he could go from serious to playful in an instant.

"What? Why are you looking at me that way?" she asked.

"I'm wondering if now is a suitable time for our first kiss. We've got the faint mist hanging just above the Corrib River, the lovely lights of St. Nicholas." He gestured all around then looked skyward. "Damn! No moonlight!"

Delk couldn't stop a smile from spreading across her

face. "I can do without moonlight just this once. But you'll have to work on that for next time," she teased.

"I'll do me best," said Pather, leaning in to her. His jacket was cold, but his lips were soft and warm. In Pather's embrace, Delk's head filled up with all the *good* things life had to offer—a totally handsome boy who seemed to *get* her, the new friends she'd made, the beautiful scenery of Ireland, and her recently acquired sense of independence. *This is what happy feels like,* she thought to herself. It was a feeling she'd lost track of a long time ago—until Ireland, that is. They stood on the bridge and kissed for a long while, but like everything else about her trip here, the moment still passed much too quickly.

"My sister will accuse me of ditching her," Pather whispered. Delk was reluctant to leave, but she didn't want to make a bad impression on Katie. She'd already done that with another of Pather's sisters.

"We should go," she agreed.

The whole way back to McGarvey's, Delk's heart soared—it was as though Pather had filled it with helium and handed it to her on a string. When they reached Shop Street again, she spotted Katie and Seamus. They stood outside McGarvey's looking rather impatient.

"Finally!" said Katie, punching Pather's arm.

"Dear God!" said Pather, rubbing the place Katie'd hit. "It's all her fault," he teased, pointing to Delk. Delk punched his other arm, although *not* as hard as Katie.

The four of them laughed and headed up the street to a "chipper."

"This is our version of fast food," Katie explained when they were all seated and in the early stages of devouring fried food. "Fish and chips are brutal on the arteries, but heavenly to the taste buds!"

"You have to fit in that wedding gown, remember?" said Pather.

"And you'll be shuttin' your gob unless you want a bruise on the other arm!" Katie warned. "Speaking of bloody weddings, I think I'm going about mine all arseways."

Seamus groaned. "Here we go," he mumbled.

"I know you're sick of hearing it, but how on earth can I plan a wedding while living in London! Seamus and I are thinking it might be better to have it there."

"In London?" asked Pather.

"With no ma to help, I have to do everything myself, and we've so little money to spare for trips back and forth."

"But you're the last daughter," said Pather. "You'll break tradition if you don't get married at St. Joseph's."

"But how else can I manage it?" said Katie. Seamus quietly ate his fish and chips. Clearly, he was leaving this decision up to his bride.

"What if we all pitched in?" asked Pather. "The girls could help. They've had weddings before. How hard can it be?"

"It can be plenty hard," Delk threw in. She'd helped

Paige and her dad plan their wedding (reluctantly, of course) and she couldn't believe how much planning it took—and Paige *had* a mother, a very competent one at that!

"Thank you!" said Katie, nodding to Delk. "Our sisters have babies and jobs and houses and husbands. You and Da have the farm and Tremain. It's not like I'm the only one who's busy. I can't be a dosser and push things off on all of you."

"What kind of wedding do you want?" asked Delk. She was instantly sympathetic. After all, she'd been in the same situation herself with the whole Forest Hills thing.

"A small affair, really," said Katie.

"And cheap," Seamus threw in. Katie shot him a look.

"Modest," she corrected him. "I don't want a shabby wedding, by any means."

"I think small ones are much nicer," said Delk. "My . . . well, I helped someone with a wedding not long ago, and I think when they're too big, it's not as much fun. It just seems nicer when it's simple. More elegant somehow."

"I agree wholeheartedly!" said Katie. "And I intend to have fun on my wedding day. I don't want to run 'round biting everyone's head off and fretting over silly details."

"Exactly," said Delk. Suddenly it occurred to her. "Why don't I help you? I live right across the road, and I've helped plan a wedding before—very recently, too. And, I

have most afternoons free. I could squeeze in some wedding details here and there, no problem."

Katie's eyes widened slightly. "Oh, I could never ask
that of you, but what a generous offer. Thank you."

"Well, if you change your mind, let me know. I wouldn't
mind at all, I promise."

It was getting late, and even though Mrs. Connolly
hadn't given the S.A.S.S. students a specific curfew, Delk
sensed it was time to get back. They piled into what
Pather referred to as the Keneally clunker and drove Delk
to her hotel. Just before getting out, Delk scrawled her e-
mail address on a scrap of paper and handed it to Katie.
"Seriously, if you change your mind about needing help,
I'm willing."

Katie tucked the paper into her pocket. "Thank you,"
she said.

The four of them said their polite good-byes, then
Pather walked Delk to the hotel's main entrance. He kissed
her lightly on the lips, both of them aware that Katie and
Seamus were watching from the car. "I had a good time
tonight, Love," he said.

"Me, too," Delk replied. She rode the elevator to the
fourth floor and smiled the whole way up. Not only was
this the best St. Patrick's Day she'd ever had, it was the
best day, period. At least the best day she could remember
having in a very long time.

# Chapter Eight

After Delk and the others returned from Galway, life became a blur. Mr. Hammond packed their semester schedules with New Experiences; Delk had a long list of books to read for the Irish writers class; and Mrs. Connolly had already handed out a thick packet detailing the *final* project for the semester—and it wasn't even April yet. She still had eight weeks left in Ireland, and she refused to think about the *final* anything.

"Wait!" Latreece called after Delk. The midmorning break bell had sounded, and Delk wanted to beat the rush to KC's snack tray. Pather was in Galway working on a school project, and Delk had taken the opportunity to sleep in, which meant she'd missed breakfast. "I saw the official contract for my modeling job this morning!" Latreece squealed.

"But the mail hasn't even come yet," said Delk. Ever since her return from Paris, Latreece had shared every minute detail of Le Papillon's offer: *The powers that be were in a meeting; it looked like they would make the offer; they were interviewing another model—an older model who could actually sign a contract; no, she didn't work out; yes, they wanted Latreece, but maybe...* It was like listening to a tennis match on the radio. Delk was trying to be enthusiastic, but at the moment she was starving!

"My agent sent an e-mail attachment. She won't send the paper copy until it's closer to my birthday. But it's in writing with my name on it! Can you believe it?"

"Congratulations," said Delk, hugging her.

Downstairs, the girls, joined by Iris and Lucy, sat huddled in a corner eating KC's moist yellow pound cake. "So do the 'rents know yet?" asked Iris.

Latreece shook her head. "I can't tell them because then they'll know I went to Paris, and if they know I went to Paris, they'll call Mrs. Connolly. And if she finds out—"

"She'll kick your ass back to Baltimore!" said Iris.

"Exactly." Latreece nodded. "My plan is to sign it, *then* tell them. Maybe I'll just fly to Paris straight from here, not even go home first. What's the point in going back

to Baltimore if I have to listen to nonstop fighting, right? But I absolutely *have* to get in shape. It takes a lot of self-discipline, you know."

"Yeah," said Iris, rolling her eyes.

"I have another surprise. It involves a certain delivery I got yesterday. Two bottles of the finest French champagne and an enormous box of chocolates, courtesy of Le Papillon. Oh, and perfume for all of you, too. If the weather's nice, we could head down to the lake this afternoon for a picnic."

"Sounds good to me!" said Delk.

"When it comes to chocolate, you don't have to ask me twice," said Lucy.

"Ditto!" Iris agreed.

By the time the girls finally met up by the lough, it was nearly four o'clock, and *not* great weather—slightly brisk and overcast. Still, it felt good to have something to celebrate, and unlike beer, Delk actually liked the delicate taste of champagne. Latreece had borrowed a large picnic basket and glasses from KC, and while Delk and Iris spread out a thick blanket, Lucy and Latreece opened the chocolates and poured the champagne.

"Here's to Latreece's success!" said Lucy when they were all seated. She raised her glass for a toast. "I wish you many years of modeling, and when you have too many wrinkles for that, I hope you become the editor at *Vogue*.

Or, a person who gets free shoes at least!" she added.

"I'll toast to that!" said Delk, tapping her glass against the others.

"I'd settle for free chocolate," said Iris.

"So *what* are your parents gonna say about all this when you finally tell them?" asked Delk.

"Well, my father will want to invest the money for me and handle all that practical stuff. He's always been supportive. He's the one who paid for my head shots and took me out on several photo shoots—until my mother found out and tried to sue him for it. She said it wasn't within his rights as a father to prostitute his own daughter."

"Jeez! She said that?" asked Iris.

Latreece nodded. "At least those first few gigs were enough to get a decent book together."

"Book?" asked Iris.

"Portfolio of the work I've done," Latreece explained. "Anyway, my mom is this wannabe feminist, full of ideas and opinions, even though she's the most traditional type of woman. You know, car pool, PTA, room mom. Who is she to judge me for not being some flaming feminist!"

"Tell her you'll major in women's studies when you go to college," said Lucy. "Or join NOW."

"What's NOW?" asked Delk.

"National Organization for Women. The original bra burners," Lucy explained. "Just tell her modern feminism is really about choices. Whether you're a model or an astronaut,

it's all about the freedom to pursue what you love."

"Go Hillary!" Iris joked.

"Why is it that mothers are so annoying?" Lucy continued. "When my mother wants to find out how my brothers are doing, guess who she calls? Me! Like I'm their personal attendant or something. I can't wait to go to college next year. Maybe then she'll have to keep an eye on them herself for a change."

"Try having a teacher for a mother," said Iris. "Scary! Daily lessons taped on the fridge for when I get home from school!"

"What kind of lessons?" asked Latreece.

"Like see if you can work out this math problem. Or, read this article on sperm whales in *National Geo*. I'm homeschooled *and* school-schooled."

Delk felt her mood sinking. This picnic had turned into a mother-bashing session, and Delk had heard enough of that from Julie and Rebecca and all her other friends back home. She plucked up a handful of clover and searched for one with four leaves. "What?" she asked, looking up. The girls had gotten quiet, and Delk realized they were all looking at her. "What?" she asked again, feeling redness creep into her face.

"I'm guessing your mother is probably perfect," said Latreece. "All sweet with a nice Southern accent, but cool about stuff, too, right?"

Delk froze, and her face felt hot. "Something like that,"

she mumbled, and chugged the last sip of champagne. They were waiting for more of an explanation, and Delk felt trapped suddenly. She longed to race up the Tremain hill and hide in her room.

"So how come you never talk about home?" asked Latreece.

"Just not that much to say, you know. I'm not into bashing my mother the way y'all are," she replied, trying to keep the anger from seeping into her voice.

"I wouldn't call it *bashing*," said Lucy. "I love my mom. It's just that she drives me crazy. I mean if you have a mother, she's going to drive you crazy, right? It's a law of nature or something."

"You know, I think this champagne is upsetting my stomach a little," Delk announced suddenly. "Plus, I have a ton of homework, and it's a little chilly out here. I'm gonna go back now. Do y'all need me to carry anything?" The three of them looked at her blankly, but shook their heads no. "All right, see you later, then," she said, trying to sound cheerful. "And thanks for the champagne, Latreece!"

The whole way up the Tremain hill, Delk fumed. She thought of the lavish care package Lucy's mom had sent just days earlier—a pretty white box decorated with stickers and filled with nail polish, favorite snacks, dental floss, books, and fashion magazines. And Iris's mom had signed her up for sailing lessons for the entire summer because her daughter had casually mentioned in an e-mail that it

was one of the few sports she hadn't tried yet. Delk could somewhat understand Latreece's frustrations, but even so, her mother was only trying to do her job, make sure her daughter didn't become some stick-figure tabloid star, and Delk happened to think it was entirely possible to be a room mother *and* a feminist all at the same time.

Angrily, she climbed the stairs to the second floor, went into her room, and locked the door. Of course, the girls would know something was wrong, and Iris would probably come check on her later. She'd behaved strangely, and it wasn't fair, she knew.

Delk snatched Wooby off her pillow and lay down on her bed. She closed her eyes and thought back to one summer several years ago when she'd gone off to camp. Her mother had just started dialysis then, and Delk hadn't wanted to leave her. She was terribly homesick until her mother shipped her a whole box of Jell-O chocolate pudding and double-stuffed Oreos. Inside was a note: *Sweets for my sweetie. I miss you.* Delk still had the faded scrap of paper taped to her mirror at home—that is if Paige hadn't taken it upon herself to redecorate her bedroom, too!

Delk squeezed Wooby tighter and closed her eyes. "I miss you, Mom," she whispered. "I miss you so much."

"Hey, Cowgirl, let me in!" Iris was practically kicking the door down. Delk blinked at the clock and realized she'd snoozed right through her second meal of the day. "KC sent supper up for you," said Iris when Delk opened the door. She stood there in sweats holding an overloaded tray, enough to feed Brent, Trent, *and* Lucy, Delk noticed. "You missed breakfast this morning, too. What's up? You sick or something?"

"Just tired, or maybe it's PMS," she lied.

"Or SMP. Sinclair Missing Pather," Iris teased, but Delk didn't feel like making jokes.

She took the tray from Iris and set it down on her dressing table. "Thanks for getting this."

"Want me to hang with you?" Iris offered.

"I'm fine, really. I think it's all those early mornings and late nights. I just need to sleep."

"Okeydokey, Cowgirl. I'll be right next door. You sure you're okay?"

"I'm *fine!*" said Delk.

"Okay, okay. See ya later," said Iris.

Delk tried to eat a few bites, but the tray of food blurred behind her tears. She turned off the light, climbed into bed, and cried *under* her pillow—so no one would hear.

The next morning Delk felt a little better. Maybe it was the extra sleep that'd improved her mood, or the fact that it was Friday and Pather was coming home. Whatever it was that had lifted her spirits, she had no intention of

overanalyzing it. She tugged on her bathrobe and made a to-do list for next week's New Experience—sheepshearing at the Keneally farm.

Delk was glad students were allowed to select their own New Experiences, and it would be fun to see Pather in all his sheep-farming glory—the precise reason Delk had chosen such an activity in the first place. She could just imagine Julie and Rebecca's grossed-out reactions to such a task, a thought that made her miss them suddenly. Quickly, she pushed her Nashville friends out of her head. She wasn't about to let herself go gloomy again.

"Delk! Delk! Let me in!" Lucy called through the door.

"What? What's wrong?" asked Delk, flinging it open.

Still wearing her pajamas, Lucy hurried inside, and Delk shut the door behind her. "It's Latreece. I just saw Mrs. Connolly drag her off downstairs."

"Literally?" asked Delk.

"No, not like by the ear or anything, but she had this really mad look on her face. I think she knows about Paris."

"Oh God. She'll kick her out."

"I know," said Lucy.

Iris knocked once and barged right in. "Mornin', ladies. Are we feeling less PMS-y today, Cowgirl?" she teased.

"Mrs. Connolly knows about Paris," said Delk.

"Oh no." Iris's face fell. "She's screwed. Oh, man, she is totally screwed."

After getting dressed, they headed down to breakfast and ate in silence. Latreece never showed. Mrs. Connolly taught her seven o'clock Irish writers course, but Latreece wasn't there. She didn't come to any of the other classes either. Delk was beginning to wonder if Latreece had *already* been sent home. After lunch, she and the others headed up the stairs and banged on Latreece's door. No answer. Just then Mrs. Connolly came up behind them.

"She's not here," she said firmly. The five of them looked at one another. "Her parents are flying in from the States. She's gone to meet them in Galway. I suspect you all know the situation." Mrs. Connolly turned sharply on her navy heel and took off down the hall.

"She's in deep," Lucy whispered.

"Up to her eyeballs," Iris agreed.

"Think she'll have to give up all that modeling stuff?" asked Trent.

"Probably," said Delk. "It sounds like her parents have come to escort her home."

"It's stupid!" said Brent. "I mean, she'll be eighteen soon. That's old enough to vote or fight in a war if she wants. What's the big deal about posing for a magazine?"

"I guess we'll just have to wait and see what happens," said Lucy.

"I guess so," Trent replied, although he was staring at Iris when he said it.

• • •

The weekend was spent speculating about Latreece. On Friday night, they all went to Bird's, Pather included, and discussed the possible outcomes of her situation. On Saturday, they headed over to Connemara National Park for the day and hiked up Benbaun, one of the official Twelve Bens, according to the guidebook. Latreece was very much on their minds. By Sunday, Delk had sworn off talking about it. She accompanied Pather to St. Joseph's Church, and afterward, they had lunch in Letterfrack, just the two of them.

"There's a special place I'd like to show you on the way home. It's a bit of a hike. Do you mind?" asked Pather.

"Not at all," said Delk. Obviously, she was hoping to stretch the afternoon out as long as possible. Hand in hand, they trudged up a grassy knoll. The ground was littered with what looked like confetti, but up close Delk could see the little spots were colorful flowers—deep purple, pale yellow, white, and lavender, and the tree buds had opened slightly—an Irish spring.

Delk heard the rushing of the stream before she actually saw it. A thick carpet of moss lined either side of the cool, tumbling water, and there were smooth gray rocks and lush plants. "It's beautiful!" she said. "Like a painting!"

"I thought you'd like it," said Pather. "I used to come here when I was younger. I love to read, and I could never get any peace at home, so I'd tuck my book in my jeans and come here. No one could ever find me."

"Oh, this would be a heavenly escape! And the ground is so soft." She sat down and ran her hand across the plush green moss. "I like to read, too, but I read in my room or outside on the patio. No one ever bothers me, though. At least they didn't use to. I guess with a baby around that'll be different."

"Not in the beginning," said Pather expertly. "Babies sleep a lot. You'll hardly know he's there until he cries. Hopefully, the little one won't get colic. That's dreadful. When's the dote due?"

"Sometime in mid-July. I can't remember the exact date. So what do you like to read?" asked Delk.

"When I was a kid, I loved Tolkien. Lately, I've been reading Thomas Hardy—when I have time to read," he added.

"No way! I love him! *Return of the Native, Tess, Jude the Obscure.*"

"Ah! Poor Jude and those children of his! And Tess—a girl who did absolutely nothing wrong!"

"Don't *even* get me started on Bathsheba Everdene!" Delk cried.

"Hey, I brought something to show you. It's a picture of my ma." He handed Delk a tarnished silver frame no larger than a credit card.

"She looks exactly like Katie," said Delk.

"'Tis amazing the resemblance of all three of you," said Pather. "Da even mentioned it that day we picked you and

Iris up at the airport. I must say, though, I'm very glad we're not related!" Delk handed him the frame, and he tucked it back in his pocket.

"Me, too. Because it would make doing this extremely inappropriate." She leaned in closer and kissed him.

"Yes, it would," said Pather, kissing her back. She was nestled against him now and enjoying the sounds of early April—the stream rushing beside them, the birds chirping overhead.

"So who else do you like, besides Thomas Hardy?" Delk asked.

"I like you," said Pather, wrapping his arms around her tightly.

Delk's heart thumped so rapidly she was certain Pather could hear it. "I like you, too," she replied.

"You're blushing," he teased.

"So are *you*!"

By the time they returned to Tremain, it was getting late. She was hoping Pather might join her for dinner, but he had chores still to do, and homework. From the foyer Delk could hear KC shouting orders to one of the cooks. From the sound of things, they were having roast chicken for dinner, and Delk was starving. "Delk! Up here!" She glanced up to see Lucy peering over the balcony. "She's back!"

Like a rocket Delk shot up the stairs and followed Lucy

down to Latreece's room. The door was open, and Delk could see she was packing. "Oh no!" said Delk. "You're leaving?"

"My parents are upstairs talking to Mrs. Connolly right now. My mom's so mad. She's making me go back to Baltimore, where she can 'keep an eye on me.'" Latreece made air quotations.

"What does your dad say?" asked Delk.

"He's willing to let me stay, willing to let me sign the contract, too. It's my *mother* who refuses to let go! She acts like I'm ten or something! That woman drives me crazy. Absolutely nuts!" said Latreece angrily.

Delk took a deep breath. She couldn't decide whether to say what she was thinking or keep it to herself. Finally, she decided to go for it. "Maybe your mom's just sad. Sad that you're growing up and moving so far away."

"Or sad that she can't control me anymore! You have no idea, Delk," said Latreece sharply.

"I have an idea that a mother who drives you crazy is better than no mother at all," Delk replied.

"What do you mean, Cowgirl?" Iris prodded.

Delk sighed. "My mother died two years ago." She uttered the words much the same way she skipped stones—all at once and with her eyes closed.

"How? What happened?" asked Iris, her eyes round with alarm.

"I'm so sorry," said Lucy.

"Me, too," said Latreece. She stopped her unpacking and sat down to listen.

"It's okay. Y'all didn't know. She died of kidney disease. Or, well…I mean it started out as strep throat, only she didn't know she had strep. She just thought it was a cold. My mom wasn't the type to run off to the doctor. Anyway, by the time they caught it, she had kidney failure. She was on dialysis for a long time, but she died waiting for a transplant."

The girls stared at her. "You never said anything," said Iris. "You didn't tell us."

"I know. I'm sorry. I just…well, my life back home is pretty complicated. My dad remarried way too soon. To someone much younger. Only ten years older than me!"

"Oh God," said Latreece.

"And they're having a baby. And she's totally changing everything about our house. It's like she's trying to purge my mother out of it somehow. She's not evil, just clueless. So, I came to Ireland and let you all think my life was wonderful. I thought it'd be easier that way." She glanced at Latreece's suitcase and felt a sharp pang at the thought of her friend leaving before the semester was over. "It's just that I can sort of understand why your mom doesn't want you to live in Paris. It's horrible to feel like you might lose someone forever—and even worse to have it actually happen. Latreece, I really think you should tell your mom you're sorry. Forget the Paris thing for a while. For now, concentrate on getting her to let you stay here in Ireland."

"Delk's right," Lucy agreed. Iris nodded.

Latreece stared at her perfectly manicured nails. "The problem is I'm not sorry for going to Paris."

"Your mother doesn't have to know that," said Lucy.

"Exactly," Iris added.

"Just go talk to her. Apologize to Mrs. Connolly, too," said Delk, all but shoving Latreece out the door.

Latreece clicked off down the hallway in her spiky-heeled boots, and Delk was left with Lucy and Iris. Like two sad-eyed puppies, they blinked at her. She felt exposed suddenly, as if all her problems were naked and dancing indecently around Latreece's room. A part of her wanted to snatch back the truth and hide it again. Another part felt relieved not to have to pretend anymore. Either way, her mother wasn't just dead back in Nashville. She was dead here in Ireland now, too. Gone forever, no matter how far Delk ran.

# Chapter Nine

Delk couldn't help but stare at the clock all through her Monday-morning classes. She had her sheepshearing New Experience later today, and she couldn't wait! Okay, she could wait for the sheepshearing part, but she was excited to see Pather, at least. Besides that, she *needed* to get away from Latreece, Lucy, and Iris for a while.

Ever since she'd told them the truth, they'd been too solicitous. "Are you sure you're okay?" Iris must've asked fifty times. "Can I get you anything?" Latreece inquired every time she passed by Delk's door, as if Delk had a bad cold and was in need of chicken soup. And it wasn't so much *what* Lucy said, it was the puppy dog look she tossed Delk's way every time they met. They meant well, Delk knew that, but she'd never understood why people thought pity was the appropriate response to tragedy.

The dismissal bell rang, and Delk bolted for the door. "Hey, Cowgirl. Wait!" Iris called after her.

"I'm going to the Keneally farm," Delk reminded her.

"You're okay then? Want me to walk with you?"

"I'm *fine*," said Delk, "but I'd be better if y'all would stop asking me that every five seconds. Did Latreece's mom make up her mind yet?"

Iris shook her head. "They're having a family powwow in a few minutes. Hey, is that offer still good?"

"What offer?"

"For that makeover you mentioned a while ago. I don't want it right this second, but would Saturday work?"

"Saturday's fine," said Delk. "But why'd you change your mind?"

"No reason. Just did. Keep your fingers crossed for Latreece." Iris waved her off.

Delk rolled her eyes. This was probably some sympathy ploy the girls had cooked up. Poor Iris was actually willing to suffer through a makeover just to cheer her up. Delk bounded down the stairs, rounded the corner, and noticed Trent standing near her door.

"Hey, Delk, got a minute?" he asked.

"I'm late for my New Experience," Delk replied. Trent

followed her into the room and watched while she smeared on lip gloss. "What is it?" asked Delk, shoving the wand back in the tube.

"Where's Iris?" he asked.

"She might've been going to the library. I'm not sure. Why?"

"No reason." He shrugged.

"Trent, I really do have to go."

"Do you think Iris would go out with me?" he blurted. Delk felt her mouth drop open. "I wanna ask her out, but I think she thinks of me as just some dude. I asked Lucy about it, but you know Iris better than anybody. I don't wanna, you know, piss her off or anything."

"You want to ask her out?"

"Yeah, I was thinkin' we might do something this Saturday?"

"So what did Lucy say?"

"She said I should ask you."

The pieces were starting to fall into place—Iris's sudden request for a makeover, the way Trent followed Iris around between classes sometimes, sat next to her at meals, trudged all over Galway on St. Paddy's Day looking for Iris snacks (and missed half the parade because of it).

"I think you should definitely ask her out," said Delk, running a brush through her hair. She switched off the light and edged Trent out the door.

"One more thing," said Trent.

"Yes?"

He rubbed his chin and glanced up at the ceiling. "It sucks about your mom."

Delk smiled up at him. She'd always liked Trent. He was funny, slightly crazy, and very much an individual—sort of like Iris, now that she thought about it. "Trent, that's the best condolence I've ever heard," she said.

"Sorry, I meant—"

"No, I *mean* it. It really is the best one I've heard—the most accurate anyway." Delk shut her door. "Ask her out!" she said and hurried down the stairs.

The Keneally barn was enormous, and its doors were flung wide open to let in the spring sunshine. Birds flitted from rafter to rafter and chirped playfully overhead. The cows mooed out in the pasture. Through the open door, Delk could see them swishing their tails and chewing their thick tongues.

"You're here!" said Pather. Delk watched as he trudged through the muck, carrying a bale of hay. Effortlessly, he tossed it into a stall then pulled off his gloves. "I would hug you, but I'm a mess. Sorry." He smiled. "The manky life of a farmer."

"I'll take a hug anyway," said Delk. He wrapped his arms around her, and Delk couldn't help but notice he smelled

like a boy who'd been playing outside all day—fresh air with a little sweat mixed in. She liked this smell even better than his just-showered one.

"I told them," Delk announced proudly.

"Told them? Oh, you told the girls about your ma?" Delk nodded. To most people it wouldn't seem like much, but for her it was a fairly huge accomplishment. Pather hugged her again. "That's grand, Love. And how did they react?"

"They're being sort of overprotective."

"It'll take time. My guess is by the end of the week, they'll be givin' you hell again. Well, at least this old ewe will give you hell. No sympathy from that girl, I can tell you."

"I have a confession to make. I don't know the first thing about shearing sheep."

"Naughty girl. You didn't do your preliminary research! Preliminary research is a vital part of the overall New Experience," Pather teased.

Delk recognized this line from Mr. Hammond's syllabus. "It was a busy weekend," she reminded him.

"Ah, so it's *my* fault you didn't do your homework?" Delk nodded and grinned up at him. "Well, it's understandable, I suppose. I mean, look at me. Irresistible in every way." He laughed, glancing down at his dirty clothes.

Delk studied his farmer garb—mud-encrusted work boots, a red flannel shirt, grass-stained overalls. Her stomach dropped as if on a roller coaster. Pather Keneally was the most ruggedly handsome boy she'd ever laid eyes on. Yes, he *was* irresistible! She wondered what Julie and Rebecca would say if they could see her now.

Her Nashville friends preferred the Abercrombie look on guys—distressed jeans and hoodies, forty-dollar T-shirts, flip-flops even in winter. Pather didn't need professionally distressed jeans. He was perfectly capable of wearing out his clothes all on his own—the *real* way, with hard work. She felt a surge of affection for him suddenly. An awkward silence fell like a curtain between them, and Delk felt as though her thoughts were being broadcast on a loudspeaker. She blushed.

"Well, even though you didn't do your homework, I'll do me best to mold you into a national sheepshearing champion," said Pather, easing them past the awkwardness.

"National champion? You're kidding, right?" Pather shook his head. "You mean there's a contest for sheep shearing?"

"You're learning from the best!" Pather teased. "I was a finalist last year in Galway."

"No way!" She could hardly believe the things people won prizes for. "Back home there's a contest for the prettiest mule," Delk confessed.

"Sounds like an oxymoron to me." Pather laughed.

"I'm not kidding. There's a little town not far from Nashville, and they have something called Mule Day. My

parents took me once. The mule gets a crown and every-thing."

A sheep bleated noisily inside one of the barn stalls. "That's our cue, I suppose. They must be getting restless. I'll shear the first sheep," Pather explained. "You watch, and then you can try your hand on the second one." Delk hadn't noticed, but there were actually two sheep bleating in the stall.

The sheep's coat looked more like dreadlocks than wool—matted and dirty and thick. Pather pulled something that resembled her dad's electric razor off the shelf and plugged it into an outlet. He wedged the docile creature between his knees and started buzzing around her backside.

"You shear a bit off the back," Pather shouted over the noise, "and then a little off the head. Take some off the feet. You want it to come off in one big piece," he explained. Delk watched as he made expert strokes with the shears. The sheep was perfectly behaved, no bleating or moving around. While Pather sheared her back and belly and sides, the polite creature sat on her rear end, like a client at the hairdresser.

Pather switched off the clippers and led the animal back into its stall. Clearly, he was some sort of champion; the entire procedure was finished in about five minutes. He flung the wool out across the barn floor. "When you're done, you roll it up like a sleeping bag," he explained.

Carefully, Delk examined the product. Underneath the dirty-looking dreds was pure cream-colored fleece, like her Aran Island sweater.

"It's pretty," she said, "and so soft."

Pather led the second sheep out of the stall. "Ready?" he asked, handing her the shears.

Delk wedged the creature between her thighs, just as she'd seen Pather do, and turned on the shears. She had to keep stopping and starting because the animal wouldn't stay still. The ewe bleated and squirmed. At one point it bolted and ran through the barn, its partly sheared wool dragging on the floor. Delk and Pather chased it down, and Pather held it steady while Delk attempted to finish the haircut. When the job was finally done, Delk's fleece didn't look at all like Pather's. Instead of one large piece, hers was in various clumps—a big clump here, a little clump there.

"I can't believe I ruined all that wool," said Delk. "I'm sorry."

"Oh, 'tisn't worth much anyway," said Pather.

"It isn't?" asked Delk, surprised.

"At the moment the wool market isn't much to brag about. People wear synthetic blends now. We started raising cows because of it. Da thinks we should give up sheep farming altogether or start selling off lambs."

"Sell the lambs?" asked Delk.

"For meat," Pather explained. Instantly, Delk thought of

the motherless twins. "I have some other ideas," Pather reassured her. "I've been researching the wool insulation market. You can actually use sheep wool in place of traditional insulation. It's environmentally friendly, too. No harsh chemicals, no ill effects from handling. It's quite a clever idea, but Da is still skeptical."

Delk had never considered the complications of farming. "It must be a constant struggle," she said.

"*Life* is a constant struggle," said Pather, shrugging his broad shoulders. He grinned at Delk and took her cool hand into his own warm one.

"You Irish always seem so...so...positive...so happy. Always laughing and dancing," said Delk enviously. "I wish I could be more like that."

"You're talkin' like a tourist now," said Pather. His face was serious.

"I'm sorry," said Delk quickly. "I meant it as a compliment, not a stereotype."

"No offense taken," said Pather. He sat down on a mound of loose hay and pulled Delk down beside him. "What you say is partly true, but I get cheesed off that the world thinks of us as simpletons. All sheep and leprechauns and sunny green pastures, just like in the brochures, but there's an awful lot of rain here, and it's cold at times, bone-chilling damp cold, but *that's* never in the brochures." Delk knew firsthand that this was true. "Life is no easier here than anyplace else, and the Irish have suffered a great many atrocities over the centuries—war, persecution, famine, poverty. Da always says that those who've known great sadness have a better appreciation for happiness. Those who've seen death know the value of life. That's really what we Irish are about, at least that's what I think anyway."

Delk shredded a piece of hay and mulled the words over in her head. "What if you're stuck in between?" she asked finally.

"What do you mean, Love?"

"Like if you've known sadness and seen death, but you can't get to the part about happiness and life?"

"I suppose then you have to get a bit stubborn, push past the sadness."

They sat for a while longer in silence. There was something hopeful in Father's words, something that rang true. Delk felt the urge to call her father suddenly, to tell him she loved him. He'd remarried, that was true, and he'd allowed Paige to take over their lives, but he was still Delk's father, and they had an entire history together that Paige would never share whether she changed the wallpaper or not.

"Thank you," she said, hugging Father tightly.

"For what?" he asked, putting his arm around her.

"For being here with me. For listening."

"Any time." Father grinned. The sunlight caught his green eyes, and Delk noticed there were flecks of gray and blue in them.

Pather walked her back to Tremain, but he wouldn't come inside. "I'm in need of a shower," he said. "I was wonderin' if you might like to come for supper Saturday night. It'll be crazy. It's Da's birthday, and the entire family's coming. Katie's coming home, too."

"Oh, to plan the wedding?" asked Delk.

Pather nodded. "She's a fright these days. Nothing's done, and she's over a cliff about it."

"I told her I'd help!" said Delk. "Look, please tell her I don't mind at all. I'd be much better helping her with a wedding than helping you shear that sheep."

"Well, let's hope so!" Pather teased. Delk shoved him playfully.

"Tell her! Okay?" said Delk, walking backward toward the door.

"I'll tell her," Pather promised. "I suspect she'll be e-mailing you."

Before dinner, Delk tried to call her dad, but the answering machine picked up. She decided to send an e-mail instead. The pleasant *ding* sounded when she logged on, and there were two messages waiting:

---

**From:** PearsonSinclair@email.com

**To:** DelSinc@email.com

**Subject:** Pregnancy

Hi Delk——

I thought you should know that Paige is in the hospital. She's experiencing symptoms of premature labor, so the doctors have put her on some drug to prevent the baby from coming. The good news is the labor has stopped. The bad news is the drug makes Paige feel dreadfully nauseated. I'll keep you posted. Hope you're having fun. I miss you terribly, though.

Love,

Dad

------------------------------------------------

**From:** Katie.Keneally@email.com
**To:** DelSinc@email.com
**Subject:** Wedding

Hi Delk,

Remember me? Pather's sister? Hope all is well. I am writing to see if you're willing to help with the wedding. Since I saw you on St. Patrick's, I've planned nothing. The nuptials are now FOUR weeks away.

I would love your opinion on a few things. Would you be available to spend the day with me this Saturday? I'll treat you to a nice lunch, I promise.

Fondly,

Katie

Delk read her father's e-mail twice. She tried to picture him going through these experiences without her. A new

wife and baby, a practically new house, a new life. It was as though the two of them had been on a path that'd diverged suddenly, and they'd gone in different directions. With so many of her personal problems still looming, it was good that Katie had asked for Delk's help. She needed all the distractions she could get right now. She shut off the computer and went into the hallway. In the distance she could hear shrieks. Low at first, muffled by stone walls and wood floors, but then she recognized the voices and hurried down the stairs.

Latreece and Lucy were jumping up and down, and Iris stood watching them, a grin stretched wide across her face. The three of them turned to look at Delk. "My guess is you're staying?" asked Delk.

"Yep! I'm afraid you guys are stuck with me!" said Latreece. "Isn't it great! My mom changed her mind at the very last minute. She's still adamant about me not going to Paris." She rolled her eyes. "But I think it really impressed her that...well, that I apologized. Thanks for the good advice."

"I'm glad you're staying. I think we should make the most of it!" said Delk.

"Ditto!" Iris agreed.

Just then Brent and Trent came barreling down the hallway and slapped Latreece high fives.

Delk stood back a bit. As if pasting a photo into a

scrapbook, she tried to press the moment onto her memory. Ireland was changing them, *all* of them, and in ways they couldn't see. Their friendships were changing them, too. Even if Delk wasn't on the same path as her dad, she was still in a very good place. Maybe she was pushing past the sadness after all.

Delk spent the rest of the week getting ahead. She skimmed through a few of the sheepshearing books and wrote up a detailed New Experience report for Mr. Hammond. He gave her an *A*, thankfully. She finally got around to the notes Mrs. Connolly had handed out a while ago for the final project. Her assignment was to teach an entire class on William Butler Yeats, a double disadvantage since Delk had never taught a class in her entire life, *and* she'd never read a thing, at least not that she could remember, by Yeats. Luckily, there was plenty of time to get her act together, do some reading, and come up with a decent lesson plan. It might actually turn out to be fun.

Right now there were more pressing concerns, though: how to prepare a very nervous Iris for her first official date—*ever*; how to help a bride prepare for a wedding that was only four weeks away; and how to juggle a makeover, wedding-planning session, and Keneally dinner all on the same day. Somehow, she would make it all work.

• • •

Saturday morning was beautiful—warm sunshine, nice even breezes, brilliant ethereal light shining down like great slanted ladders. Delk's mother always said someone was climbing up to heaven when the sky looked that way. She couldn't wait to help Katie. It would be so much fun planning a wedding that wouldn't impact the rest of her own life. Delk crossed the main road and headed toward the farmhouse. The sound of banging hammers pierced the quiet morning air, and she glanced around. She spotted them now, several shirtless men on top of the barn.

"Hey!" she called up to Pather, but he didn't hear her. "Hey!" she yelled again.

Pather waved and pounded in one more nail. "Give it a rest, fellas," he called to the other workers. Delk couldn't help but notice how Pather's muscles flexed sharply with the weight of the hammer, and his fair skin was slightly pink and glistening with sweat. *Was he ever sexy!* Delk thought to herself, and smiled up at him. "Off to plan the wedding?" Pather asked.

"Yep," she replied.

"I have a feeling between you and my sister, you'll have the whole thing figured out in two hours flat."

"That's about all the time we have!" Delk laughed. "I'll see you tonight," she said, and headed toward the house.

"Come in!" Katie called from an upstairs window. "I'm just finishing up."

The Keneally house was plain, all cozy function. The

breakfast dishes were piled high in the sink. The radio played, but the volume was so low it gave off a humming sound. Overhead, Katie's shoes clicked back and forth across the creaky wooden floors. "All set?" she asked when she was down the stairs.

"I'm ready if you are," said Delk.

The two of them hopped into the Keneally clunker. Katie drove past the barn and out onto the main road, and Delk turned around just in time to see Pather waving good-bye with his hammer. "I hope they get that barn finished in time," said Katie.

"In time?" asked Delk.

"That's where we've decided to have the reception." She looked at Delk and winced a little. Delk tried to picture it—not littered with hay and manure, but cleaned up and with a band and decorations and lots of guests.

"That could be a lot of fun," said Delk. Katie looked at her skeptically. "I'm really not kidding." She glanced down at her boots. "Maybe you could have a cowgirl theme." She grinned.

The first stop was at St. Joseph's, the tiny stone church she and Pather had gone to. The door was ajar, so they quietly stepped inside. Katie bowed before the shiny brass cross then knelt at the altar to pray, and Delk slid into one of the wooden pews behind her. The stained glass seemed more brilliant this morning—blues and reds and greens and whites—a kaleidoscope of color. Candles glimmered

on a small wooden rack around the periphery of the room, giving off the thick smell of wax mingled with dust. Katie crossed herself and stood. Quickly, she lit a candle and placed it beside the others.

"Ready?" she asked when she had finished.

"Shouldn't we meet with the priest or something?" Delk whispered, although there was no one else in the room.

"Father Philip knows the details already," said Katie. "It'll be the exact ceremony all my sisters had. I just came to pray for the strength to get through the next four weeks—and for my ma. It's my ritual really. I always light a candle for her when I'm home," she said. "Ma loved this little church."

"Would it be okay if I lit one, too?" asked Delk. She didn't explain her reasons, and she had no idea whether or not Pather had told Katie about her mother.

"Of course," Katie replied. "Take your time. I'll wait in the car."

Delk lit a candle and placed it on the altar next to Katie's. Under her breath, she said a quick prayer and then headed to the car. The two of them buckled up, and Katie switched on the radio. "I think we should go straight to Galway. We've got an appointment with the dressmaker at noon."

"You're having a dress *made*!" said Delk, the panic rising in her chest.

"Oh, just an alteration. I'm wearing the dress Ma and

my sisters wore. It's a bit on the shabby side now, as I'm the last girl to wear it, but Mrs. Fitzpatrick can fix it right up. I hope anyway. This is probably nothing like the weddings you're used to in America. Are they fancy?"

"Oh, they're elaborate and complicated and *stressful*; at least my dad and stepmom's was. They actually met at a wedding about a year ago."

"Sounds like they moved pretty fast."

"Record-breaking speed," Delk replied. "They met in May, married in September, and they're expecting a baby this coming July."

"That must be hard for you," Katie pointed out. "I have the opposite problem with Da. He won't *move* at all. He hasn't dated since Ma died eight years ago, not one single dinner out. It drives us all crazy, but he says in his heart he's still married. It would be like cheating or some such nonsense. It pains me to think of him all alone when Pather goes to university this fall. I mean he'll come home and all. Pather is very dedicated that way, but still..." Her voice trailed off, and the two of them were silent.

In Galway, Katie parked the car and retrieved her gown from the trunk. Unfortunately, it was covered in opaque plastic, so Delk couldn't see it. She followed Katie up Shop Street, and they passed a florist's shop along the way. Katie gasped. "Flowers! I haven't ordered any flowers!"

"Well, let's go in, then," said Delk.

A bell jingled on the front door as they entered the tiny

store, which was full to bursting with flowers—fragrant lilies, exotic orchids, drooping peonies, and brilliant purple iris. Delk spotted an arrangement of pink peonies with some sort of strange green stalklike flower she'd never seen before.

"What are these?" she asked the stocky sales lady.

"Ah, *Moluccella laevis*, of course. Also known as bells of Ireland. I love these flowers. They're hardy. They last forever, and I do mean *forever*. You can hang them upside down, and they'll dry out quite nicely. They're a symbol of good luck, too." Katie and Delk exchanged looks and put their dark heads together for a quick discussion.

"I'll give you sisters a moment to think things over," said the saleslady, and she whistled off to the back room.

Delk and Katie smiled at the "sisters" comment.

"I like that they last forever," said Katie. "A good omen, don't you think?"

"Definitely," Delk replied. "We could mix them with these"—she touched the soft pink petals of a peony—"and maybe some ivy trailing down." Her imagination was now in overdrive. She could picture the little country church overflowing with bells of Ireland—its vibrant green color giving the interior a lively, verdant feel. "And your bridesmaids could carry a smaller version of your bouquet!" said Delk, barely able to contain her enthusiasm. Just then the saleslady returned, and Delk explained her ideas again.

"We'd need to get a price for all this, of course," said Katie.

"Oh yes," Delk added. "What is your budget for flowers?" she whispered.

"I hadn't thought of it," Katie admitted. "As you're quickly learning, I haven't thought of a *lot* of things!" she joked. They waited for the saleslady's estimate. The woman handed Katie a slip of paper, and Katie's cheerful demeanor deflated.

"I'm afraid that's just for one bouquet," the saleslady said sympathetically.

"We could trim it down a little," Delk offered.

By the time they left the florist, Katie's bridal bouquet consisted of one lonely peony, a single stalk of bells of Ireland, and no ivy.

The trip to Mrs. Fitzpatrick's didn't go much better. "It's hopeless," the dressmaker said when she saw the hand-me-down gown. "These yellow places I can't do a bloody thing with! And moth holes! Jaysus! You girls should preserve this dress better if you're gonna keep wearin' the same one! I expect the grandkids'll be in here next!" she scolded. "I am not Mrs. Fitzpatrick the bloody miracle worker. You'd be better off gettin' a new one. Cheaper that way, too."

"Trim!" Delk squeaked. "We'll trim it with something. Irish lace! We'll tea-stain it to match the rest of the dress."

Mrs. Fitzpatrick gazed at Delk from across the top of her little half-glasses. "Looks like we have an optimist on our hands," she groaned.

By the time the two of them talked Mrs. Fitzpatrick into at least *trying* to fix the dress, they were exhausted. "Let's eat," said Katie when they left the shop. "I'm sick of wedding planning already."

Delk decided not to remind her how much more there was still to do. "Do you suppose we could find a café that serves *cold* Diet Coke?" Delk was feeling desperate for a taste of home.

"Of course!" said Katie. "I know just the place. I can't thank you enough for helping me," she said when the two of them were settled in a snug at a nearby café and sipping ice-cold soda.

"I just wish there were some way to get our hands on those bells of Ireland. They would be so pretty in the church. There has to be some way to get them cheaply. Maybe I can do a little research on the Internet."

"Maybe," said Katie. She had the look of one very overwhelmed bride.

"We'll make it work," said Delk. She sipped her soda and watched Katie twist her Claddagh ring nervously around her finger.

"I should've been planning for months, saving money. I just thought a simple country wedding would be a craic, you know? Nothing to fret over."

"It'll be fine." Delk smiled. "I love your Claddagh ring," she said, reaching for Katie's hand to examine it more closely. "What does it mean again?"

"The heart symbolizes love. The crown means loyalty and fidelity, and the hands mean friendship. If you're engaged like me, you wear it on the left hand, crown toward the knuckle," Katie explained. "When Seamus and I marry, he'll turn it 'round the other way. If you want to, we could walk over to the Claddagh Village where the rings were first made. It's not too far from here." Delk nodded enthusiastically.

After they'd eaten, the two of them strolled up Shop Street and Quay toward the Wolfe Tone Bridge. The streets were filled with people and various venders selling their wares. Along the way, Katie explained the story of Richard Joyce, the goldsmith who made the first Claddagh rings in that very village four hundred years ago. It was fascinating to think that these elegant pieces of jewelry were now worn all over the world. "Did Seamus give you the ring?" asked Delk.

"Oh no. It's traditional for the Claddagh to be passed from mother to daughter. My mother had so many daughters, though." Katie laughed. "When Ma died, Bevine got Ma's ring, the one passed down from my grandmother, but Ma thought of everything," said Katie. "She always did," she added. "She bought the rest of us rings when we were first born, but she didn't give them to us until we

turned thirteen. She even got one for Pather—*before* he was born." Katie smiled. "She probably thought he would be a girl, too."

"But some men wear Claddaghs, don't they?" asked Delk.

"Yes, but the one Ma bought for him is small. Besides, Pather says they're too clunky for farm work." They stopped just at the water's edge and watched the swans swim by.

"How did your mother die?" asked Delk.

"Car accident," Katie replied, gazing out over the water. "She'd been to mass. A tire blew on the way home, and she was gone. I was nineteen, Pather's age, when it happened. My brother was only eleven." She paused. "I *do* know what you're going through." Katie looked at her.

"Pather told you?" Katie nodded. Delk was glad Pather had told his sister; she was relieved not to have to tell the story again. "Does it ever...you know...get any better?"

Katie shrugged her narrow shoulders and smiled. "In some ways it does, but it's a bit like running a long race with a rock in your shoe. You get used to it, but it always hurts a little."

# Chapter Ten

Delk hopped out of the car and charged up the stairs. She had exactly one hour to help Iris with her makeover *and* get herself ready for the Keneally family dinner. She stopped by her room, changed clothes quickly, grabbed her makeup bag, and headed next door.

"Hey, Cowgirl!" said Iris. She glanced down at Delk's floral print makeup bag. "The plastic surgeon's in *there*?" she quipped.

"Shut *up*!" said Delk. "You're gonna look great. What are you wearing?" Iris had on faded, ripped jeans, a ragged Bon Jovi T-shirt, and Birkenstocks.

"You're lookin' at it," she said, opening her arms wide.

"Okay, well, that's the first thing we're making over," said Delk, pushing her way past Iris and heading straight for the armoire. She tugged open the slightly warped doors and peered inside. Empty darkness stared back at her. "Where are your clothes?"

"Over there." Iris pointed to a small pile of dirty laundry. "And there." She pointed to her iPod hi-fi. "It was either music or clothes."

Delk shook her head. "Well, we could borrow something, I guess."

"From who?" asked Iris.

"Now just let me think. I'll be right back!" she said, and took off toward Latreece's room. She knocked loudly on the door.

"You rang?" asked Latreece.

"It's the Iris Carson makeover hour, and we need your help. Could you maybe bring down a few things that might fit her? She has nothing to wear—and that's not just some girlie excuse. She really *doesn't* have anything to wear."

"I'll see what I can do," Latreece replied. "I have a few of those oversize sweaters we might try. Iris and I are about the same height."

"Great!" said Delk, heading to Lucy's door next. "Hey, Luce. Can you get together some accessories for Iris? We're doing a little makeover before her date with Trent."

"You realize Trent will be wearing shorts, a T-shirt, and flip-flops?" Lucy told her.

Delk shrugged. "I promised I'd help."

"Okay, be there in a sec."

Delk hurried back to Iris's room. "Sit on the bed," She said, glancing at the clock. She now had only thirty minutes to complete her task. She extracted foundation, concealer, eye shadow, blush, bronzer, loose powder, pressed powder, mascara, lipstick, and lip gloss from her bag.

"You're painting the Sistine Chapel?" asked Iris.

"Very funny," said Delk, although she put the foundation, bronzer, pressed powder, and lipstick back in her bag again. "You wanted this, remember?"

By the time Latreece and Lucy showed up, Delk was trying to coax Iris into using the eyelash curler.

"What *is* this! *Fear Factor*!" Iris protested. "You are *not* sticking that thing in my eye."

"Oh, stop being such a baby!" Latreece scolded.

"That's it!" said Iris, pushing the eyelash curler away. "We're done here."

"Iris, you can't go without a little mascara and blush and lip gloss. Sit down!" Delk ordered. "We'll skip the eyelash curler. I swear, it was easier to shear that sheep!" Iris sat down again, and Delk expertly brushed her cheekbones with *Sweetheart Pink*. She dabbed her lips with matching gloss, although Iris flatly refused the mascara.

"Now we just have to fix her hair. What do you guys think? Straight? Curly? Up? Down?" asked Delk. Latreece and Lucy examined Iris's hair carefully.

"We could shave it," Iris suggested, blinking up at them. The girls ignored her.

"How's the humidity tonight?" asked Lucy.

"The humidity?" asked Iris.

"It was pretty bad, actually," Delk replied.

"Then you should definitely pull it back," said Latreece.

"Boys usually like hair down, though," said Delk. "It's sexier down."

"This is not brain surgery here," said Iris. "Just fix it so it doesn't fall in my face every five seconds."

"Back," the three of them agreed.

Latreece went to work on a casual up-do while Lucy and Delk tried to piece together a suitable outfit. Finally, they settled on the least dirty and ripped pair of jeans and an oversize sweater from Latreece's collection. Lucy loaned her a great pair of earrings, but Iris's old Birkenstocks would have to do—no one had size-twelve shoes.

"I still think you should be going out with somebody way cuter than my stupid brother," Lucy teased when they were done. "You sure look great! Have fun tonight, okay?" she said, heading out the door.

"Thanks," said Iris. "I will."

"I'd love to stick around," Latreece said, "but I'm chatting live with a Paris real-estate agent in a few minutes. I have to find an apartment."

"Want me to stay?" asked Delk when Lucy and Latreece were gone.

"Aren't you supposed to be at Pather's tonight?" asked Iris.

"Oh my God! You haven't even looked in the mirror yet. Here, come look!" Delk dragged Iris across the room. Iris stared at herself, but she didn't say anything. "Well?" asked Delk.

"You guys did a great job," said Iris, a hint of worry in her voice. "Cowgirl, how much do you think this sweater cost? I mean, what if I spill something on it or snag it or rip a big hole somewhere?"

"Are you playing tackle football or going out to dinner?" asked Delk. Iris grinned. "Okay, don't answer that. I'd say it's worth a couple hundred dollars." Iris looked as though she'd swallowed a hedgehog. "Okay, maybe not that much. Just be careful."

"Thanks, Cowgirl. You're the best," said Iris.

"Anytime," Delk replied.

Pather came to fetch Delk on foot. It was a pretty moon-lit night, and the two of them walked at a leisurely pace toward the Keneally farm. "Are you sure you're ready for this?" he asked.

"Sure!" said Delk, ignoring the uneasy feeling in her stomach. "What's everybody's name? Maybe we should go through them all before I get there."

"You want the brothers-in-law and nieces and nephews, too?" asked Pather. "Or just the sisters?"

"Just the sisters for now," Delk replied.

"Bevine and Maeve are the two oldest, only nine months apart, then there's Brigid, Laurie, and Katie. I wouldn't worry. You've relieved them from having to deal with Katie's wedding details. Chances are they all like you already."

"Except for Maeve," Delk reminded him. "I still feel so—"

"Oh, would you stop frettin' over that? Maeve's hauled all of us home mangled, puking, or both at least once. Just be yourself. How could they not love you?" said Pather, kissing her lightly on the cheek. Something about the "love" word coming out of Pather's mouth made Delk's stomach catch slightly.

The farmhouse was overflowing, *literally*. Children spilled out onto the lawn, men sat on the steps drinking beer and telling jokes. Delk could smell the food even before she saw it. "Hi, everyone," said Pather, "this is Delk." The men stopped their talking and greeted Delk.

"It's nice to see you again, Delk," said Mr. Keneally.

"Nice to see you, too," Delk replied. "Happy birthday. Nice to meet all of you."

Inside, Pather's sisters were bickering over where to put the casseroles and desserts and side dishes. "I say we put the main things in the dining room, and leave the desserts out here in the kitchen," a tall redhead was saying.

"But the kids'll have it all gobbled up in no time!" a strawberry blonde protested.

"I want you all to meet Delk Sinclair, my friend from Nashville, Tennessee," Pather shouted over them.

"Hey! She's my friend, too!" Katie waved from across the crowded room. She sat at the kitchen table with a little girl on her lap. The two of them were flipping through a bridal magazine. The other sisters stopped their arguing to offer polite hellos.

Dinner was served haphazardly. Half the casseroles were in the dining room, the other half in the kitchen. The desserts were stacked on top of a china cabinet to keep the children from stealing into them, and two rhubarb pies were badly mangled in the process of getting them down again. And there was a birthday cake, of course.

On the sofa Delk sat wedged next to Pather and tried to balance a plate on her lap. She thought of Iris suddenly and wondered how her date was going.

"So tell me about your family," Maeve was asking her. She sat in a corner chair and leaned in closer to hear above the raucousness.

"I'm an only child," said Delk, "but that's about to change," she added. "My stepmom's expecting a baby

in July. She's been having trouble with premature labor, though. They've got her on some sort of medicine."

"Oh, that's magnesium sulfate! I had that. So did Bevine. Horrible stuff. It kept the baby from coming too soon, though. So your folks are divorced?"

"No, my mother died a couple of years ago. My dad remarried last September."

"I'm so sorry," said Maeve, touching Delk's hand softly. "We lost our ma, but I'm sure Pather's told you already." Delk nodded. "It's a difficult burden on a family, large or small. But, we make the best of what we have, I suppose. Whatever family you have 'tis a blessing. And you'll be a sister! How old are you?"

"Seventeen," Delk replied.

"Oh, there's sixteen years between Pather and Bevine. At the moment, Bevine and I are both thirty-five—Irish twins, you know—but she'll be thirty-six soon. Pather's was the first nappy I ever changed, and he had the diaper rash like you wouldn't believe!"

"Shut your gob, Maeve!" Pather warned.

"Oh, the stories I could tell," Maeve teased. "We'll have to go to the pub one night, just the girls. We could *all* fill you in."

"Don't listen to a word of it!" said Pather. He reached across Delk and playfully squeezed the place just above his sister's knee.

"Okay! Mercy!" Maeve cried.

"Do you see what I have to put up with! I hope you'll be slightly more kind to that innocent sibling of yours, Delk!"

After the dishes were somewhat cleared away, and the children had settled in front of the TV for a movie and ice cream, the men started up a game of cards, and Pather joined them. The Keneally sisters and Delk pored over old family wedding albums.

It was late when the evening finally broke up, past midnight. The children were like sacks of beans by the time they were hauled out. Pather drove Delk back to Tremain in the Keneally clunker. When they pulled up to the castle, they could see Iris and Trent in the headlights. Iris was wearing her own clothes again, and Trent was shirtless and barefoot. The two of them were playing catch with lacrosse sticks. Judging by the look of things, it hadn't been a romantic evening.

"Hey!" Pather and Delk called to Iris and Trent.

"Hey!" they called back. Obviously, Delk would get the details later, but it looked like they were still friends at least.

Pather walked Delk to the castle door, and the two of them stepped inside the dim foyer. "Thanks for puttin' up with all that nonsense tonight," he said, laughing, and Delk noticed the faint crinkles at the corners of his eyes. He looked like his father just then.

"It was great," she said. "You're so lucky. I mean to have a family like that. And there are so many of you."

"That's without the aunts, uncles, and cousins," he added. "You were a hit. They all liked you, I could tell. I knew they would."

"I'm glad," said Delk. He leaned down and kissed her, and they lingered in each other's arms for a while.

"Good night, Love," said Pather finally.

"Good night," she replied, and headed up the stairs.

She was tucked in bed by the time Iris knocked on her door. "You 'sleep?" Iris called.

"No, come on in," Delk answered, switching on the light. She could see Iris's makeup was completely gone, and the carefully messy up-do had melted into sweaty strands. Even without the makeover, Iris still looked pretty—full flushed cheeks, bright eyes. She was definitely in better shape than all Delk's personally trained, gym-obsessed friends back home. Maybe a makeover hadn't really been necessary, after all. "So how was the date?"

"He kissed me!" said Iris, checking to see that the door was closed all the way. "He actually *kissed* me."

"But you were playing lacrosse when Pather and I drove up," Delk pointed out.

"I know. We went to dinner. Ate gobs of food. Came home to the castle. Kissed a couple of times. Then I said I needed to move, and Trent knew exactly what I meant. Can you believe it? So we bummed lacrosse sticks and a ball off Brent and played catch. Oh, and I have a confession. I was too freaked out to wear Latreece's sweater. It probably cost more than my parents' mortgage. And after I took off the sweater, well... the makeup kinda seemed out of place."

"So what'd you do?" asked Delk.

"I washed it off, threw my hair in a ponytail, and went as myself," said Iris proudly. "I don't wanna jinx it, but I think it's the real me Trent's interested in."

Delk felt like a proud mother sitting there listening to Iris talk about her night. They were all making strides here at Tremain. Every single one of them, Delk thought excitedly. After all, that night she had told Maeve the truth about her Nashville life, and she didn't cringe once.

# Chapter Eleven

It was another Monday morning, a rainy one, and Mrs. Connolly stood at the front of the room with her arms crossed over her chest. Obviously, she was irritated. She'd intended to spend class time discussing final projects, but there wasn't much to discuss since Lucy was the only student who had started hers. Mrs. Connolly was now going around the room, singling kids out. "So, Delk, what about you?" she asked, her lips pressed together in a grimace. "Surely *you've* done some reading on your topic at least?"

"Uh...well, actually, I haven't had a chance for that

yet, but I was planning to start later today. We do have six whole weeks left," she pointed out.

"That's six weeks until you go *home*," said Mrs. Connolly. "We'll spend the last two weeks of the semester on final projects, and your day to teach a lesson on Yeats is May twenty-third—about *four* weeks away. This information is in your packet. Haven't you read it?"

"Oh, I read it," Delk replied, "but I'll look over it again, I promise." Mrs. Connolly nodded and moved on to another student. In truth, Delk had only skimmed part of the packet, and in spite of Mrs. Connolly's efforts to make her feel guilty, there were far more pressing concerns in her life right now. Katie and Seamus's wedding was only two weeks away, and the to-do list was so long, she didn't even attempt to write it all down anymore! Admittedly, it wasn't her wedding, Katie wasn't her sister, and she wasn't even a member of the bridal party, but Delk still wanted things to be perfect. She understood Katie's motherless situation. She'd be in the same boat herself one day, and besides that, she'd missed out on having her own Forest Hills presentation party. Katie and Seamus's wedding seemed like a good substitute.

Ever since the night at the Keneallys, they had *all*—busy sisters and brothers-in-law included—pitched in to get the wedding details in order. And, in two weeks' time, there'd been progress. The invitations were done. Seamus

and Katie were sending snail mail ones to the guests who didn't have access to e-mail. The task of getting bridesmaid dresses was cleared out of the way. Katie's sisters had gone to a boutique and purchased beige linen skirts and elegant white blouses. The groomsmen agreed to wear dark, conservative suits.

There were so many other things left to do, however. Delk was still searching the Internet for wholesale bells of Ireland. Pather was trying to persuade a few of his old friends to get their band back together so they could play for the night. Due to rain, the barn roof still wasn't finished. And St. Joseph's, for all its pretty details, needed a thorough cleaning. Delk and Pather had gone to see Father Philip about this, but the man merely shrugged his shoulders and said, "The altar guild isn't what it used to be." Apparently, a cleaning service hadn't been in the budget for years.

To save Katie a long-distance call, Delk phoned Mrs. Fitzpatrick to check on the dress, but all the seamstress would say was "Marry in May, rue the day!" Delk tried to press her on exactly what that meant, but she hung up. Panic-stricken, Delk called Katie in London. "Oh, that's a silly Irish saying!" said Katie. "We're a very superstitious people at times. May is a lovely time to marry." When Delk hung up, she realized her heart was banging out a rhythm: *Marry in May, rue the day.*

Reluctantly, Delk dragged her daydreamy mind back to

Mrs. Connolly and the final project. Judging by the serious expressions on the faces around her, the woman was saying something important. "Um...excuse me," said Delk. "I'm not sure I caught that last part."

"I *said,* based on the lack of progress among you, I'm cancelling classes for Thursday and Friday," Mrs. Connolly said firmly.

"All classes?" asked Brent.

"Yes," Mrs. Connolly replied. "I want you to take this project seriously, and I know your other instructors agree."

"You mean we don't have to show up for classes those days at all?" asked Trent.

"What I *mean* is that all of you will use Thursday and Friday and the weekend for research. If you will actually *look* at the packets, you'll see that for most of you some travel is necessary. Obviously, I will be in charge of the hotel arrangements and transportation and such, but we'll go over all that later. In the meantime, I expect that by tomorrow's class, you'll have some progress and plans to report. You are dismissed!" she said before the bell even rang.

After classes were over and the lunch dishes had been cleared away, the six of them sat around the table and read over their packets.

"So this is basically like one big final exam," said Latreece. "We'll have a grade for each class, but then the

final project will be averaged in equally with all our other grades."

"Exactly," said Lucy. "This isn't just Mrs. Connolly's assignment. I mean, I guess she's in charge, but it counts toward your grade in *every* class."

"Jeez!" said Iris. "So if you screw this up—"

"You could ruin your overall grade for the semester," said Lucy.

"I can't afford to screw anything else up," said Latreece. "One little mistake, and I'll have to listen to my—" She stopped herself and glanced at Delk. "Well, let's just say life wouldn't be pleasant."

Already Brent and Trent's assignment packets were a mess, marked up and spread out all over the table. Delk wondered how they'd manage next year without Lucy around to keep them organized.

"Says here me and Trent are supposed to hike the Twelve Bens and do our own documentary about it, something other hikers could actually use to plan a trip. Tremain has a reporter's camera and everything. Mr. Hammond's the adviser. You think he'll teach us how to use everything?" asked Brent excitedly.

"Sure," said Trent. "If not, we'll figure it out on our own. It's a pretty cool idea. I mean at least Mrs. Connolly gets it that we're not the library types." He grinned and looked at Iris.

"So what about yours, Delk?" asked Latreece.

"I have to research Willliam Butler Yeats, go to his home, Thoor Ballylee, and teach a lesson on him. Y'all had better look interested when I'm teaching, too—and you boys better not give me any trouble, or I'll put you all in detention!" Delk teased.

"Cowgirl, you do have this teacher way about you. All those little lists you make—and that obsession with ironing everything."

"What's an obsession with ironing got to do with teaching?" asked Delk.

Iris shrugged. "Just seems like a teacherly thing to do. I'm researching the spawning salmon in case anyone cares."

"Disgusting," said Latreece. "By *yourself*?"

"No, some professor in Galway's letting me tag along with his college students."

"Thank God I didn't get that one!" said Latreece. "I'll be examining the fashion trends specific to Irish women. I get to visit all the cool shops in Dublin, *and* I have to create my own magazine with real articles and pictures and everything. And, Lucy and I can travel together, which will be nice."

"You're doing fashion, too?" asked Delk, feeling somewhat envious. It would be fun to go to the city with the other girls.

"No, I have a project on the Book of Kells."

"What's that?" asked Delk.

"It's a manuscript that dates back to AD 800. It was

written and illustrated by Celtic monks. It's housed in Dublin at Trinity College."

"Sounds hard," said Brent.

"So wait," Delk interrupted. "All of you get to go with other people, and I'm stuck by myself? How did that happen?"

"I wouldn't worry," said Lucy. "Mrs. Connolly's not gonna just send you off totally alone. Knowing her, she's probably planned your itinerary down to the last bathroom break, and I'm sure she has you staying someplace with people she knows."

"Yeah, but *I* don't know them," Delk complained.

"You didn't know us at first either," Iris reminded her.

On Thursday just before lunch, Delk packed her duffel bag, checked and rechecked the itinerary Mrs. Connolly had given her (Lucy was right—every last detail had been planned), and read over a description of the place where she'd be staying. She grabbed her book of Yeats's poems, as well as her map and guidebook, and headed down to the main road to meet the Connemara bus. Most of the Tremain students had left much earlier that morning, although Brent and Trent were so excited, they'd bolted a day early, with specific instructions from Mrs. Connolly to call the second they arrived at their first stopping point. If Delk were their teacher, she'd have made them wear a GPS tracking device.

Delk stood at the end of the drive and listened to the hammers pounding across the road. She'd wanted to tell Father good-bye, but since her father called with a Paige-and-baby update, there wouldn't be time for that now. She could see the bus grinding its way up the road.

On the bus, she tried to read several more Yeats poems, but it was a bumpy, smelly ride, thanks to a washed-out road and an *un*washed man who occupied the seat next to her. Delk closed the book and let her thoughts drift. For some reason, her mind was stuck on the day she'd spent in Galway with Katie and the Keneally family dinner that same night.

"Thoor Ballylee, miss," the driver shouted, jarring Delk.

Quickly, she slung her backpack over her shoulder and stepped off the bus. "Wait!" she called, realizing she'd left her guidebook. "Wait! I left my...Damn!" she cursed. "I hate Yeats!" she mumbled as she pressed up the road. Maybe that would be the title of her lesson: *I Hate Yeats!* A few hundred yards ahead, she spotted it, a square tow-erlike building with four windows trimmed in green and stacked one on top of the other. Lush ivy hung off the side of the building, and a river flowed directly past. If Delk had her guidebook, she could record the name of the river. As it was, she'd make a note and look up the fact later.

Inside an office tucked just behind the tower, Delk pur-chased a ticket from the young receptionist at the desk. Judging from the stack of poetry books beside her, she

was a student herself. "Thank you. I hope you enjoy your time here," the girl said, and handed Delk her change. "To leave here is to leave beauty behind."

"Uh, yeah. Thanks," said Delk, closing the door behind her. "Whatever *that* means," she mumbled under her breath. She pulled out her notebook but put it away again. Maybe it was better to really look at things first before trying to jot down a bunch of facts.

It was pretty here. She had to give Yeats that much at least. Poetic pretty, actually. A narrow, spiral staircase led to the tower's top floor. Delk climbed it with ease and stood gazing out the open fourth-story window. Below, the nameless river flowed past, and a heron landed on some rocks just beside the arched bridge. Everything smelled green and warm—the trees, the grass, the ivy. Begrudgingly, she let the images wash over her, and her bad mood subsided a little.

A few of Yeats's letters and books were preserved under a glass case. Delk took out her notebook and leaned down to examine them more closely. She spotted it then, a tattered letter that said, *To leave here is to leave beauty behind.* She jotted down the words in her notebook and climbed a ladder to the tower's roof. A stiff breeze ruffled the trees, blowing the morning's raindrops from the top leaves down to the lower ones. Delk thought it sounded like applause. The heron took off to some unknown destination. The river rushed past. Even when the world seemed still, it was forever moving, changing—much like Delk's family.

Ever since the Saturday with Katie in Galway, Delk was beginning to wonder about her relationship with Paige. Katie and Paige were similar in some ways—same age, well educated, newly married (almost). If it was possible for Delk to get along so well with Katie, wouldn't it be possible to get along with Paige, too? And if Pather could be close to Bevine and Maeve, both sixteen years older than he, wouldn't it be possible for Delk to play an important role in her baby brother or sister's life?

Maybe all Delk had to do was *decide* to make these things priorities. She'd been so busy resisting Paige and the new baby, but maybe she'd be happier if she just accepted them, gave them both a chance. Maybe there was no other choice. Suddenly Delk had an idea for her lesson: *The Places We Love and How They Change Us!*

Delk snapped lots of pictures from various angles and recorded her feelings about the place in her notebook. She was eager to learn about Yeats suddenly. Maybe Thoor Ballylee had had a similar effect on the famous poet, and if so, she could certainly relate!

When she was finally finished with her tour, she headed back to the Thoor Ballylee office. Mrs. Connolly had made arrangements at a local B&B, and she'd even written down the directions for getting there (it was within walking distance), but the information was in Delk's guidebook, which

was still on the bus. "I'm looking for the Yeats Inn?" she asked. "Could you point me in the right direction?"

The young receptionist looked up from her book. "I live there," she said. "I'll take you myself if you don't mind waiting another half hour."

"Oh, uh...that's okay. I'll walk if you'll tell me where it is. Thanks for the offer, though."

The girl climbed off a squeaky chair and opened the front door. "It's just down the road a piece. Half a mile or so. The second drive to the left. You're the only guest for the night," she explained. "My parents run the place, but they're away. I'll be there shortly, but you can go on in."

The girl, whose name turned out to be Isolde, arrived half an hour later, just as promised. She showed Delk to her room, offered a snack of tea and scones, and informed her that supper would be brought to her room at 8 P.M. Delk spent the rest of the afternoon and most of the evening poring over Yeats poems and reading up on his life.

Around ten, Isolde tapped on the door. "Is there anything else I can get for you tonight?"

"Oh, no thank you," Delk replied.

"So how's Mrs. Connolly?" Isolde asked, leaning against the door.

"You know her?" Delk replied.

"She and my mother taught school together when they were young. Mrs. Connolly is my godmother, actually."

"She didn't tell me that!" said Delk.

"Well, she's pretty professional. Doesn't like to mix personal with business, I guess. She always sends her students to stay with us whenever there's one worthy of Yeats."

"Worthy of Yeats?" asked Delk.

"She's a huge fan of the poet and of Lady Gregory, his good friend. She only gives this project to talented students—her words exactly. *Don't* tell her I told you! I assume you'll be going to Coole Park tomorrow? Lady Gregory's estate?"

"Yes." Delk nodded, still wondering why Mrs. Connolly had assigned her Yeats.

The next morning Isolde called Delk down to breakfast. The small, wobbly table was covered with a cheerful linen table cloth, and in the center was a vase of fresh wildflowers. As usual, Delk was starving. She grabbed a hunk of thick brown bread and piled her plate high with fruit and eggs and bacon. "I'm surprised to see you eat like that," said Isolde. "I thought all American girls were on diets."

"Not this one," Delk replied. "This is absolutely delicious. Thank you."

After breakfast, Isolde drove Delk to Coole Park. They exchanged e-mail addresses, and Delk waved good-bye and headed toward the entrance. She picked up a few pamphlets and skimmed over them. First on her list of things to see was the Autograph Tree. According to the brochure, it was customary for well-known writers who

visited Lady Gregory to inscribe their initials on the towering copper beech tree.

Delk took a few pictures of the autographs—W. B. Yeats, George Bernard Shaw, Sean O'Casey, J. M. Synge, among others, but it was difficult to get a good shot. A large metal fence encircled the trunk to prevent other visitors from adding their own initials to the list.

Delk hiked through the Seven Woods, Coole Park's nearly four-mile nature trail; she sat by the lake and watched the swans glide past; she studied the ancient sundial and tested its accuracy by standing on the stone slab marked APRIL. Throughout the day, she read Yeats poems: "The Winding Stair"; "Coole and Ballylee"; "The Wild Swans at Coole," and others. Late that afternoon, as she made her weary way back to the bus stop, she noticed steam rising off the lush green lawn. *To leave here is to leave beauty behind,* she thought, feeling grateful suddenly that Mrs. Connolly had selected her for the Yeats project.

Delk returned to Tremain on Friday night. She was tempted to take a nap, but she decided to head up to the computer room for a while instead. There was more research to do, and now that she was on a roll, she hated to quit. Around 2 A.M., she climbed into bed and drifted off, but she was awake again by six.

Just before lunch Delk decided to call home. It was still early in Nashville, but her dad had never been a late sleeper. She waited anxiously while the phone croaked out its...

third...fourth...fifth ring. Finally, the machine picked up. *You have reached the*—"Hello. Hell-o." Her father's voice interrupted the recording. He sounded sleepy, and Delk could tell he couldn't figure out how to switch off the machine. She waited patiently. Technology was not her father's strong suit.

"Hi, Daddy. It's me," she said when all the beeping had finally stopped. "How's Paige?" she asked. "And the baby?"

"Paige came home yesterday. The baby's fine, and Paige is on bed rest for the remainder of the pregnancy."

"Is she still nauseated?" asked Delk.

"No, but she's definitely sick of staying in bed. No other choice, though."

"Can she talk?" asked Delk.

"Sure, hold on a sec."

"Hi, Delk," said Paige a moment later. She sounded groggy, and all the perky energy she was typically so full of had seemingly disappeared. "How *are* you?"

"I'm fine," said Delk. "The more important question is how are *you*?"

"I'm just happy the baby's okay. That's definitely all that matters. This protective mother instinct is pretty intense." Paige took a deep breath and let it out again. "Delk?" she asked.

"Uh-huh," Delk replied, waiting, although for what she wasn't sure.

"I...well...I was an idiot to start this renovation. I knew you didn't want me to, and I plowed right ahead anyway. I wasn't doing it to be mean; I hope you know that. I guess I thought I could walk in here as Panacea Paige with my energy and enthusiasm and cheer everybody right up—a fresh coat of paint, some new draperies, and you and your dad would snap out of your grief. I'm sorry."

"It's okay," Delk replied.

"No, it's not," said Paige firmly. "The thought of something happening to this baby..." Her voice cracked. She took a deep breath and started again. "Well, it makes me realize it would take a very long time to get over something like that. And, everything has happened so soon." There was a long pause. "Listen, I'm not allowed to do anything around the house now anyway, and I was thinking maybe when you get home, well...we could work on this project together. Heck, we can put things back like they were before, if you want."

"Things won't ever be like they were before," said Delk.

"I know but—"

"No, Paige. It's okay. I wanted to hang on to my mother's house because it felt like that was the only place where I could still feel her—you know, *with me*. But I'm starting to realize that she's not just in that house, she's...well, she's sort of everywhere I go. Sometimes, when something really funny happens, I hear Mom's laugh inside my head, not in a weird psycho way or anything, but in a good way. It's like she's living under my skin somehow."

"Maybe that's how it works," said Paige. "For a while children live under their mother's skin. Then one day in the future, the mother lives under the child's."

Another Tremain student stood outside the room, waiting to use the phone. Reluctantly, Delk said her good-byes and hung up. She climbed the stairs to her room and thought ahead to the summer months—her backyard with its lovely pool, her mother's fragrant garden. By the time she returned, it would be in full summer glory. Maybe moving forward wasn't such an unimaginable thing, after all. Maybe there was hope for the Sinclair family just as there had been hope for the Keneallys.

# Chapter Twelve

"What? *What?* What do you mean it isn't ready?" Delk heard Katie yell into the phone. It was the day before the wedding, and obviously Mrs. Fitzpatrick hadn't finished the dress yet. "I realize that, but I should've had it three days ago!" Katie's face was red, a jagged blue vein bulged in her forehead, and her voice had taken on a bridezilla shrillness. Delk grabbed the phone.

"Mrs. Fitzpatrick, this is Delk. I'll be over in an hour or so to pick up the dress," she said, and hung up. "Katie, you have a bath to take, nails to polish, a rehearsal to go to. Just…well, at least try to stay calm. Okay?" Katie nodded. Tears had gathered in her eyes, but so far they hadn't spilled over. "Now go upstairs and—"

Pather burst through the door. "What's all the bloody screamin' about?" He looked first to Katie, then to Delk.

"Oh, she was just talking to the seamstress," Delk explained.

"For the love of God, Katie, we could hear you at the barn. You sound like a mentaler." Katie covered her mouth and darted out of the room. "Wha? What'd I do?" asked Pather.

"I need you to drive me to Galway," said Delk.

They made it to the tiny shop in record time and found a parking spot just up the street. "I'll wait in the car," said Pather.

"No, you won't! I'm not going in there *alone*!" said Delk.

"Oh, all right," said Pather, climbing out of the car. Reluctantly, he followed Delk into the shop, where Mrs. Fitzpatrick sat at the foot of a dingy-looking dress form, a row of pins pressed tightly between her lips. She was hemming a skirt, which Delk took to mean Katie's dress was finished—or Mrs. Fitzpatrick had simply given up.

"Well, it's the most hideous weddin' dress I've seen in me life!" she said when the last pin was in the skirt. "I told Katie she should get a new one. Don't you Keneallys dare tell anyone I had a thing to do with it, hear? If you do, I'll be ruined!" Grunting, she rose to her feet, then she

ducked behind a dull brown curtain, and within seconds she was back again with the dress. Carefully, she hung the garment bag by the register. "Good luck," she said, and disappeared behind the curtain again.

"Is she coming back?" Delk whispered to Pather.

He shrugged. "I don't know."

"Um...Mrs. Fitzpatrick...uh, what about the charge?" Delk called. There was no answer except for the voices on a television.

"Let's get out of here," Pather whispered.

"We have to pay her!" said Delk. She slipped around the counter and peered behind the curtain. "Mrs. Fitzpatrick, I hate to bother you again, but we haven't paid for this yet."

The woman sat facing the television, her back toward Delk.

"I've warned them *all* about that dress, and not a bloody one of 'em paid me any mind. All those lovely girls traipsing down the aisle lookin' like Mary Hick. Jaysus, I'm glad this is the last Keneally girl! Now go, will you? I've a program to watch," she said, raising the volume on *Fair City*, an Irish soap opera.

Delk and Pather stood on the sidewalk outside the shop and tried to think what to do. "She's off her nut!" said Pather.

"Who's Mary Hick?" asked Delk.

Pather laughed. "Mary Hick is just an Irish expression. It means out of style, old-fashioned."

"Oh," said Delk. "Here, hold this. Up high so it doesn't touch the sidewalk." She handed Pather the heavy garment bag. Carefully, she slid the plastic off and examined the gown. The moth holes had vanished. Some of the yellowed spots had been removed altogether; others were camouflaged with delicate Irish lace. The sagging bodice had been completely reshaped and embellished with an elegant ruffle to enhance Katie's small chest. The once-full skirt had taken on a sleek modern look, trimmed down so as not to overwhelm the petite bride's frame. Mrs. Fitzpatrick had even added a train. Delk was stunned. "She's an artist! An absolute artist!" she said, zipping the bag up. "And she didn't charge Katie a thing."

The whole way back to the Keneally farm, Delk was so excited she could barely breathe. It was a beautiful day, warm spring sunshine, aquamarine sky. Maybe the wedding day would be just like this one—perfect. And now she could safely deliver the perfect wedding dress, too.

"I was wonderin', Love," said Pather. "Would you be interested in going to see the Cliffs?"

"Cliffs?" asked Delk distractedly.

"Cliffs of Moher, I mean. I know you haven't been yet, and we should go before you leave." Delk's heart squeezed up tight at the word *leave*. "We could stay with Aunt Myrna, my mother's sister. She doesn't live far from the cliffs. It would be...em...well, she has enough room and everything."

Delk glanced at him, and she could see his face was red. "I would love to go," she replied.

"Good. Then I'll ask Aunt Myrna about it tomorrow at the wedding."

At the crack of dawn the following morning, Delk slipped into a pale blue dress then crouched on the floor and felt around under her bed for her carry-on bag. It still contained the strappy heels she'd decided to pack at the last minute. Clearly, there'd been no need for them until today. "Yuck," she said, slapping at the dust bunnies. She unzipped the bag and noticed the playing cards, the ones she'd snatched from the junk drawer so many weeks ago. What was she thinking bringing those? She'd never liked card games, not even Old Maid with her mom when she was little.

If Delk ended up with the old maid, she used to fume. If her mother ended up with it, Delk said the game was stupid; clearly, her mother wasn't an old maid. Plain as day, she could see the scene—just the two of them sitting in front of the fireplace, a bowl of popcorn between them. *It's supposed to be fun, Delk!* her mother would say, laughing.

Memories, Delk had noticed, sprang up in the most unusual ways, happy little gifts—as long as you didn't let the sadness creep in.

It was early yet, the sky just barely light, and there was

only the one lamp shining in the Keneallys' front window, the one they left on all the time. Maybe no one was up yet. Before Delk had a chance to knock, Mr. Keneally flung the door open. "Thank Jaysus you're here!"

"Oh! You scared me half to death!" said Delk, clutching her chest.

"Dear girl, I'm sorry. But...well, *look* at this!" he cried, moving out of the way so Delk could see. "Some delivery boy brought them an hour ago, said you'd ordered them off the Internet."

Delk stepped into the room. "Oh! *Oh!* They came! I forgot! Well, I didn't forget. I mean...I just didn't think anyone could get them."

"What'll we do?" asked Mr. Keneally helplessly.

"Gather up every vase, bucket, and pitcher you can find. Where's Katie?"

"Still sleeping, I'm afraid. 'Twas a bit rowdy at the rehearsal last night."

"Don't wake her. Let it be a surprise," said Delk.

Quickly, the two of them loaded the Tremain van, which the Keneallys were borrowing for the day, and headed over to the still-dark church. Mr. Keneally switched on the lights, and Delk could see *someone*, probably Katie's sisters, had cleaned the place top to bottom. The linens were crisp and white, the silver polished and gleaming, the candles fresh, their wicks still coated with a fine film of wax. And now, with so many bells of Ireland, Delk could

hardly believe how elegant it all looked, and for so little money—$1.25 per stalk, far less than the florist in Galway! There must've been two hundred stalks of the brilliant green flower, but since Delk had barely spent any of the money her father put in her account for the semester, she could easily afford this for Katie and Seamus. It was the best wedding gift she could think of!

Back at the Keneally house, Katie was crying. *Again.*

"Oh, it's exquisite!" she sobbed, and Delk watched helplessly as mascara streaked her flushed cheeks. It was the gown that had prompted this latest batch of tears. "She is such a kind woman!" she went on, touching the delicate fabric lightly with her hands. "A friend of Ma's from school years. And so generous. I can't believe she wouldn't charge for this." Her face crumpled. "I'll bet she didn't charge any of my sisters either, and they never even told me."

"Okay, I know," said Delk. "But you've got to stop. You're ruining your makeup, and it's almost time to leave for the church. You're not even dressed yet!"

The farmhouse was already filled to the brim with family and friends, every guest invited, judging from the noise level, and they were toasting! At this rate, they'd all be sloshed before they even *got* to the church, although Delk supposed it didn't matter much. One of the local farmhands was driving the guests to Letterfrack on a hay wagon. The brothers-in-law had arranged for a car—a vintage Rolls-Royce—to take Katie and her father. It sat parked out front, its impatient driver alternating between polishing the already-polished hood and smoking cigarettes.

Delk and Katie had been holed up in the tight attic bedroom half the morning. "I'm scared to go down there," said Katie, her blue eyes large and damp. "I know I'll start wailing again as soon as I see all of them, especially Da. And I feel like I'm forgetting something."

"Your dress, for one thing!" Delk quipped. "Here, put it on." She held the gown while Katie stepped into it. "Are you sure we shouldn't call your sisters up for this? So they can give you advice or something?"

"No!" Katie protested. "They'll just make me even more nervous."

Delk fastened the back and fluffed out the train. She scrutinized every detail, but there were no flaws that she could see. "You're perfect. Absolutely perfect!" Katie rolled her eyes. "Come look if you don't believe me." With some trepidation, Katie followed her to the full-length mirror.

"Seamus won't even *recognize* me," she said.

"Your bouquet! I'll go get it. You wait right here. Don't move. And definitely *don't* sit down!" Delk warned.

The house all but bulged with so many perfumed bodies packed too tightly together. Delk squeezed her way through the crowd and into the dining room, where Pather was standing guard at the china cabinet.

"We've got to get these people out of here!" he shouted above the noise.

"That's your department!" Delk shouted back at him. "I'm trying to keep the bride from drowning herself."

"Is she *drinking*?" asked Pather.

"No!" Delk laughed. "She's crying over everything."

"You look perfectly lovely today," said Pather.

"And you're perfectly handsome." Delk kissed him lightly on the lips.

"I wish I could sit with you at the wedding, but I'll be up front with all the other groomsmen."

"I won't be sitting anyway. I'm the fill-in photographer until Seamus's brother can take over after the ceremony." Delk plucked Katie's bouquet off the dining room table and started toward the stairs.

"Wait!" said Pather, grabbing her wrist. Delk looked up at him.

"What?" she asked.

"Nothing, I just wanted another look at you."

Delk raced up the stairs again and opened the bedroom door. "I remembered what it was!" said Katie.

"Remembered what *what* was?" asked Delk, shutting the door behind her.

"I have to pee," said Katie.

"*That's* what you forgot!"

"I should go before the wedding. It'll be hours before

I'll have another chance." Delk groaned and unzipped the dress again.

On the way to the church, a rainstorm passed directly over them. "Marry in May, rue the day!" Mr. Keneally shouted out the window as the Rolls swished past the hay wagon. Pather drove the Tremain van, which was packed with bridesmaids and groomsmen and Delk, who was snapping pictures like a paparazzo.

Soon everything was in order: the guests were pressed shoulder to shoulder in the gleaming pews; Seamus and his dark-suited groomsmen waited patiently at the front of the church; the bridesmaids performed their step-together-step-together walk in perfect sync with the organist; and Father Philip stood ready and waiting, prayer book in hand.

A hush fell over the crowd when Katie and her father appeared in the doorway. "Jaysus, Da! Would you look at all these flowers!" said Katie, shattering the silence. The crowd laughed, Katie cried again, and Delk snapped another picture.

That afternoon at the reception, Delk and Pather made more trips from the Keneally barn to the Tremain kitchen than either of them could count. As fast as KC could prepare the food, the wedding guests devoured it—crab cakes, roast beef, lamb, oysters, salmon, and more side

dishes than Delk could keep track of. Finally, the band started up, and the guests refreshed their drinks and headed to the dance floor. Delk sprayed disinfectant while Bevine wiped down a large table in preparation for the wedding cake.

"Bevine, you've worked my girl hard enough today. She needs a drink and a dance!" As if it were the finest champagne, Pather presented Delk with a Diet Coke.

"Thank you!" she cried. A fast song was just ending, and the band launched into an Irish waltz. Pather led her to the dance floor. Delk did her best to follow Pather's lead, but she felt shy all of a sudden, as if all eyes were on the two of them. After a quick glance around the room, she realized her instincts were right—all eyes *were* on them!

"Why are they watching us?" she whispered.

"They're not watching *us*. They're watching the *belle* of Ireland," he teased.

"You can dry the flowers, you know," Delk reminded him. He laughed and pulled her closer. "Seriously, why is everyone staring?"

"I suppose it's because they've never seen me in love before."

Delk stopped and looked at him.

"Perhaps they didn't think I was capable of it." Pather picked up the beat again, and Delk's heart waltzed right into her throat.

Just before the tune ended, Mr. Keneally cut in and

twirled Delk around as if she were weightless. He was a fabulous dancer, and his eyes twinkled with mischief at the sight of Pather standing alone on the sidelines. "Let me show you how a waltz is *really* done!" he shouted in his son's direction. Mr. Keneally guided Delk and soon her feet were right in step with his. "It's been a pleasure having you in Ireland, my dear!" Mr. Keneally shouted in her ear.

"Thank you!" she replied. "I love being here." She was determined to keep things in the present tense.

"And you were so generous to do so much for Katie and Seamus. You made this a special day with your lovely flower contribution. I've never seen so much green in all me life. And that's saying quite a lot coming from an Irishman!" He laughed. The music was winding down, and Delk could sense Mr. Keneally was getting ready for a big finish. On the last note, he dipped her to the ground and swept her up again. "I hope this trip to Ireland will be the first of many for you, dear girl." With that, he kissed her cheek.

"I hope so, too, Mr. Keneally," Delk replied.

# Chapter Thirteen

Delk tapped on Iris's door. "Come in," Iris yawned. She was sitting on the edge of her bed in sweatpants and a Bon Jovi T-shirt. "Toss me those socks, will ya?" She pointed to a rolled-up ball in the corner. "The floor's too cold to get them myself."

"Oh, please," said Delk, hurling them at her head. There was another knock at the door.

"Unless you're KC with a breakfast tray, go away!" Iris teased.

"We came to see if you guys are busy after lunch," said Trent. The triplets stood pressed together in the doorway.

"Me and Brent want a do a dry run of the documentary."

"Yeah, we need a sample audience," Brent agreed. "This semester grade has to be a GPA booster. Spring semester junior year and all."

"There's a power meeting, and I'm not invited?" said Latreece, pushing her way through the Devonshire barricade. "How insulting!" She looked pretty in her swirly pink robe, and it was hard to tell if she was headed *to* the showers or just getting back. She flopped down in the chair and folded her long legs under her.

"They want us to watch their video," Delk explained.

"I'll watch," said Latreece, "as long as somebody will help me with one last photo shoot for my magazine. That's actually what I was coming to ask."

"Don't look at me!" said Iris. "*I'm* not wearing makeup again."

"As long as y'all promise to listen with rapt attention during my Yeats lesson today, I'll watch," said Delk. "And, I'll help with the photo shoot, too, but it'll have to wait till Pather and I get back. We leave for our trip today."

"We'll make ya look good, Cowgirl, don't worry," said Iris.

"Okay, if I don't share my news, I'll burst," said Latreece, jumping off the chair. "I now officially have an apartment in Paris! Can you believe it?"

"No way!" said Lucy.

"I just put the deposit down last night. Or, I should say

Le Papillon put down the deposit. Since I don't have any money of my own yet, they gave me an advance. And you guys are officially invited to crash with me anytime. In fact, I say we do next summer at my place. Invite Pather, too," Latreece added and winked at Delk.

"Are you serious? I'd love to go to Paris!" said Delk. "All that shopping and culture."

"And the Louvre. I've always wanted to go there!" Lucy agreed.

"And French fries! And French toast!" said Iris. "Listen, I hate to break up this party, but I'm hungry."

"We have to start looking at our calendars before we leave Ireland. Otherwise, we'll never do it," said Latreece. "And the flights are cheaper if you book well in advance."

"Then I'd better book mine tomorrow," said Iris.

Even with all her planning and rehearsing, a whole hour of teaching seemed daunting. Delk wondered how Mrs. Connolly could do it day after day. And there were so many things to consider: *Would she have enough material to cover? Would there be too much? And what would she do if everybody looked bored?* Delk was too preoccupied to eat, so she left her friends in the dining hall and headed up to the classroom early. She wasn't sure what to do with herself when she got there, so she sat down at her desk and pretended to read over some notes.

She glanced up when Mrs. Connolly entered the room, and the woman frowned at her. "Teachers should always greet their students before class. Go stand at the door and say hello," said Mrs. Connolly. *Strike one,* Delk thought. She hadn't even started, and already she'd made a mistake. Obediently, she followed the woman's instructions. "Hi. Good morning. Hey. Hello," she said, feeling stupid. One right after the other, her classmates filed into the room.

Brent and Trent were the last to arrive. "Good luck, Cowgirl," Trent whispered. Delk smiled at him. Ever since he and Iris started going out, he'd called her *Cowgirl.*

She put off starting the class as long as possible. She wrote the day's date on the chalkboard, tinkered with the computer, glanced over her notes again. "You may start now, Delk," said Mrs. Connolly. The students looked at her expectantly, and the backs of Delk's knees began to sweat. Her heart raced. Her mouth felt dry. She glanced at the clock—*fifty-five minutes* of torture left. Iris winked and gave a surreptitious thumbs-up, and Lucy flashed one of her supersized smiles. It was all the encouragement she needed to get started.

"Okay, well. Um... I'm doing my presentation on William Butler Yeats, and to be honest, I'd never read anything by him before this—*ever.* I wasn't exactly enthusiastic about my assignment, and when I first started to work on it, I

wanted to call the lesson *Why I Hate Yeats.*" A few students laughed, and Delk's tension eased somewhat.

"Anyway, I went to his summerhouse a few weeks ago, and I started reading his poetry, and I changed my mind. I don't hate Yeats. In fact, now I really like him." She glanced at Mrs. Connolly. "I'll start with a PowerPoint presentation just so y'all can see the house and everything." Delk clicked through the photos of Thoor Ballylee and explained the highlights of the poet's life. The students were actually paying attention, a good sign. Next, she read aloud "The Winding Stair" and pointed out its connection to Thoor Ballylee.

"I want you to take a few minutes and think about a place that's influenced you in some way. It could be a place you loved or a place you hated." Delk was getting into a groove now. The backs of her knees were no longer sweating, and her heart had stopped pounding. Strange as it was, she was actually starting to enjoy this. "You don't have to write a poem or anything. Just take out a sheet of paper and describe the place and explain your feelings about it. Try to consider how it influenced your life." She glanced at the clock. "Um...you have five minutes to do this," she added.

Five minutes felt like thirty standing there at the front of the classroom. "Okay, now, if I could ask for volunteers. Um...would somebody like to share?" Lucy, Brent, Trent,

Iris, and Latreece threw their hands in the air (they were definitely trying to make her look good), and Delk almost lost it. She glanced back at Mrs. Connolly again, and she could've sworn the woman was biting back a smile. Delk called on Latreece first.

"This is rather corny, but I did just have five minutes. Okay, mine's about Paris." Latreece grinned. "I know all of you find that shocking. Anyway, the streets smell of bread, and the cafés are crowded with people having leisurely lunches and real conversation. The women make high fashion look easy. Paris is a place that makes my heart beat faster. It's a city that makes me feel more determined than ever to reach my goals. I hope I live there forever. I also hope my friends will come visit me." She glanced up at Delk and smiled.

"Thanks," said Delk. "Okay, Trent?"

"I picked Ireland. Being in Ireland and having the freedom to travel...well, it makes me realize how the traditional college scene isn't cool for me. I'd just be some loser poser in a regular college. I'm gonna need to move and see places. Maybe distance learning or something." Delk nodded.

Iris raised her hand again. "I'll keep it short and sweet. Ireland made me even more of who I already was," she said.

Mrs. Connolly was scribbling something down in her

notebook, and Delk worried she'd let the discussion get too far off track. She felt bad not calling on Brent and Lucy. "Brent, Lucy, would y'all like to go?"

They shook their heads, and Lucy nodded toward the clock. Delk realized there were only fifteen minutes left.

Delk tried to speed things up without being obvious. She flew through the shots of Coole Park, and read the poem "The Seven Woods." She gave a brief explanation of Lady Gregory and Yeats's friendship, and she was right in the middle of "The Wild Swans at Coole" when the bell rang. Helplessly, she stood there as the S.A.S.S. students drifted out of the classroom. Had she taught them anything? she wondered. Yeats deserved a lot more than just an hour.

"Way to go, teach!" Iris whispered on her way out the door. Delk shrugged and began packing her things up.

"When you're finished, come by my office so we can go over the evaluation," said Mrs. Connolly, and she was out the door. In seconds she was back again. "Ms. Sinclair?"

"Yes, ma'am?" asked Delk. *Please, please say something nice!* she prayed.

"You have chalk on your nose." Mrs. Connolly winked.

Delk knocked at Mrs. Connolly's office door, but no one answered. There was a perfectly good chair in the hallway, but she couldn't possibly sit still now. Instead, she paced back and forth and wrung her sweaty hands. She *felt* she'd done a good job, and her classmates seemed okay with her lesson. Still, Delk could find a million things wrong with it; most likely, Mrs. Connolly could, too.

She spotted her teacher at the end of the hall. Her navy pumps sounded severe against the bare floor. "Sorry to keep you waiting, Delk," she said, and unlocked the door. The office looked exactly as it had the last time Delk was here—stacks of papers, half-dead plants, stained coffee cups. Mrs. Connolly cleared a stack of books off a chair and motioned for Delk to sit down.

"So, what was your impression of today? Were you satisfied?" Mrs. Connolly asked, and sat down at her desk.

Delk had a quick debate inside her head. *Was it better to be oblivious about her errors or cognizant of them?* Cognizant, she decided. "Well, the ending felt rushed. I wish I could've covered the other poems a little better." Mrs. Connolly nodded. "And, well...maybe we got off track a little with the discussion."

"Oh, I couldn't disagree with you more!" Mrs. Connolly interrupted. "The discussion was the best part."

"Really?" asked Delk.

"Well, the whole thing...'twas excellent. You managed to get in the meaty parts—Yeats and your travels to see the home and the poetry and so forth. Plus, you engaged your students! You helped them connect with someone far removed from their own lives—I mean the man is Irish, a poet, and he's been dead since 1939. You, dear girl,

brought him back to life today! And some of your classmates will pay attention next time one of his poems pops
up someplace. *Hopefully.*"

"Oh, well, thank you," said Delk. "Thank you."

"Not to mention that it was very brave of you to go off on
your own. I had intended to partner you with someone, but
you've matured so much since you've been here. You've
shown great progress, and I wanted to see you rise to that
next level. Traveling alone is something I force myself to
do every year. It's good for one's self-confidence. Makes a
person see that they can make their own way in the world,
*anywhere* in the world."

"Once I got used to it, it was fun being by myself. And I
wasn't really alone. I met your goddaughter. She's nice."

"Isolde is lovely and smart," Mrs. Connolly agreed. She
hesitated. "Obviously, Delk, I didn't know your mother." She
leaned forward in her chair and looked into Delk's eyes.
Something in her face softened a little. "But she must've
been a fine woman to have raised a girl like you. I'm proud
of you, dear. I hope you'll send me a line once in a while,
let me know how you're doing. I wouldn't be shocked to
see you become a teacher yourself someday. We'd have a
place here for you if you did."

One thing about stern teachers is that if you ever actually
get a compliment out of them, it truly means something.
Delk felt a little giddy. "So I guess this means I got an *A*?"

Mrs. Connolly threw her head back and laughed. "Of

course, it means you got an *A*! Dear girl, if I gushed over you any more, we wouldn't be able to fit your head through that door, now, would we!"

"Thank you, Mrs. Connolly. For everything. This has been the best semester of my life. I really mean it."

"And there are many more happy semesters ahead for you."

"I think so, too," said Delk. And the best part was, she really did think so.

Delk was positively giddy by the time she and Pather left for the drive to the Cliffs of Moher. At first, she babbled on about Mrs. Connolly's critique, but soon found herself lulled by the passing landscape. She stared out the window as a comfortable silence settled over them. She liked that about Pather. Silent or talkative, they were happy just being together.

Her mind wandered back to Katie's wedding day, and she smiled remembering the surprised look on the bride's face when she'd glimpsed the brilliant green flowers. She thought of her new friends and how kind they'd been when she eventually told them of her mother's death. So many wonderful things had happened in Ireland, and Delk had come a long way since those first gloomy days here.

Finally, Pather and Delk arrived at the Cliffs of Moher. The weather was erratic—light rain and a brisk wind one minute; warm sunshine and a swimming-pool blue sky

the next. Delk had learned not to let fickle weather stand in the way of a good time, however. She and Pather sat in the damp grass some distance from the edge of the cliffs. "This is the best day ever," she said, stretching her arms above her head.

"You say that fairly often," Pather pointed out.

"I think it fairly often." She grinned.

"So are you ready to brave the view, Love?" asked Pather. The cliffs were intimidating with their scale and height and jagged edges, and Delk wanted to work her way toward the edge gradually instead of rushing there all at once.

"I think so," she replied. Pather pulled her to her feet and led her closer to the cliffs. Layer upon layer of defiant shale and sandstone jutted sharply out into the choppy blue ocean. Puffins and razorbills and guillemots—birds Pather expertly pointed out—flew about playfully, unafraid of the height.

"Look out there." Pather pointed. "You can see everything from here. Aran Islands, Galway Bay, Twelve Bens, Maum Turk Mountains."

Like the good tourist, Delk took out her camera and began snapping pictures. An elderly couple stood not far from them, and the woman was smiling. "Want me to take a picture of the two of you?" she asked.

"That'd be great," said Delk, handing her the camera.

Delk stood beside Pather. He slipped his arm around her waist, and Delk leaned closer in to him and grinned. It was only after the couple had gone that she realized she'd forgotten to take off her glasses. The wind whipped up suddenly, and Delk latched on to Pather. "If I blow right off the edge, I'm taking you with me!" She laughed.

"I can see the headlines: 'Romantically linked couple pitched to their untimely deaths at Cliffs of Moher.' And he was just about to give her his ma's Claddagh ring. 'Twas still in his pocket when they found him. Perhaps I'll write my own Thomas Hardy–like novel." Pather's Irish eyes were smiling, and Delk was staring at him. He reached into his pocket, and Delk saw it then—a flash of gold in the sunlight. A ring just like Katie's. "I've been thinking perhaps you'd accept this as a gift from me. I mean…maybe it's sort of ridiculous since you *are* going home to America in a couple of weeks. I don't mean it as any sort of pressure. I just…well, I just want you to have it."

Delk hesitated. "Are you sure? I mean… you don't, like, want to save it for the future or something?"

"I'm very sure," said Pather. "So you'll wear it, then?"

Delk nodded. "Of course."

"Now it appears we've reached the awkward moment of deciding *how* you'll wear it. If I put it on your right hand with the heart outward, like this," he said, holding the ring just so next to Delk's finger, "it means your heart has not

yet been won. If I put it on the other way, with the heart inward, it means...well, it means your heart is taken. By me, of course," he added.

Delk laughed. "So if I love *you*, the heart should go in?"

"And if you love someone else, then *he* should give you a ring," Pather teased.

Delk pulled him close. She had never said these words to any guy (other than her father, who didn't count, of course). She looked up at Pather Keneally with his wild eyebrows and green eyes, his shock of strawberry-blond hair, his fair skin and spattering of freckles. Oh, he was handsome and rugged and all the things Delk could ever hope to find in a guy, *physically*. But, like the ring, her heart turned inward. She thought of those motherless lambs Pather had been so worried about, and the way he'd listened intently to her troubles, never telling her what to do. Just listening. And there was the gentle way he'd helped her navigate those first few weeks here. With all the courage she could muster, Delk said The Words. "I love you."

Pather slid the heart-turned-inward Claddagh on her finger. "I never expected this to happen, not in a million years," he said. "But I'm glad it did. I love you, too."

He kissed her gently, then pulled her close. She tucked her head under his chin and rested her cheek on his chest.

Delk knew she would say "I love you" again before

the day was out—not just to Pather, but to her dad, too. She'd promised to call him collect the second they arrived at Pather's aunt Myrna's house for the night. And Delk planned to talk to Paige, too. She wanted to tell her that after the baby came, she would help her with the redecorating. What did it matter in the long run if Paige changed things? Delk's mother would always be with her; Delk's father would always be her father.

"You're lost in thought again," said Pather.

Delk pulled back and clasped his hand. "I was just thinking how good it feels to be happy," she said. Her mind fast-forwarded to next summer. She pictured herself in one of those Paris outdoor cafés Latreece was always talking about, surrounded by the Devonshires and Iris and Latreece and Pather. It was tempting to fantasize about the future, especially with her departure for America right around the corner, but Delk stopped herself. For now, she would simply enjoy the present. After all, it was hard to imagine any place on Earth more magical than Ireland.